KATHE KOJA

DARK MATTER

I0637199

Meerkat Press
Asheville

Quote by Clive Barker from "The Age of Desire," from *The Inhuman Condition*. Copyright Clive Barker.
Quote by Kelly Sue DeConnick from *Captain Marvel Vol. 1: In Pursuit of Flight*. Copyright Kelly Sue DeConnick.

ISBN-13 978-1-946154-97-2 (Paperback)
ISBN-13 978-1-965740-00-2 (Ebook)

Cover design by Tricia Reeks
Book design by Tricia Reeks
Quote Collages by Tricia Reeks

Stock photos and graphics used in composite imagery and collages from AdobeStock.com, Envato Elements, and Pexels.com. Copyright belongs to the creators.

Printed in the United States of America

Published in the United States of America by
Meerkat Press, LLC, Asheville, NC
www.meerkatpress.com

The Dark Factory project combines Kathe Koja's writing and her immersive event creation for an ongoing fiction experience unlike any other.

DARK MATTER is the encore to DARK FACTORY and DARK PARK.

You can catch up with the story online, via Instagram and Facebook, or by contacting the team directly at DarkFactory.club

If you're reading this, you're already part of the experience.

DarkFactory.club

Music XR Fashion Sex always escalating!

Things move fast when you follow Ari Regon. From star manager of the legendary Dark Factory club, to managing celebrity DJ Mister Minos—who changed his handle to FRegon when they got married, keep up—through a meltdown rave called Quest Fest that sent them off to nice, quiet New York to regroup, then into a super-charged partnership with bad boy game maker Matty Bergeron and corporate titans Insomnious, to create the ultimate reality experience . . . Oh, and he's involved in a tell-all documentary film with up-and-coming auteur Sergey Kendricks. And isn't he the mascot for outlaw smoke-seller Buck Rolls? Regon's always moving from one spectacular, gritty, glittery explosion into another, crazier one. He's one of our very favorite ESCALATORS!

TOUCH THE SKY

Celebrity. Insanity. Ecstasy. Turn it up.

A FILM BY SERGEY KENDRICKS

BY YOU THIS UNIVERSE IS PROTECTED, O DEVI, BY YOU IT IS CONSUMED AT THE END.

—DEVI MAHATMYA

ONE

The bed is king-size, the sheets are midnight blue, and all at once Ari wakes—the dream of an empty hallway, miles of scrawled white walls and he runs, chasing laughter, a man's irresistible laughter—his body wakes him, with a jolt like falling.

Too early to be up but he rises anyway, naked, stretching, heading for the balcony as he shrugs on a robe, takes up his clip and a Babel cigar, pulls that door wide on hot spring sunshine and the tang of sewage, the buzz of delivery trikes in the street below. He yawns, still a little fuzzy from last night—a graduation party for Felix's latest trio of Beat Shack student DJs, Nia and Hector and Antwan, the pop-up bartender was serving champagne and bitters and everybody wanted to buy him one, everybody wanted to dance and he danced with everybody, with Antwan, he used to run with a boy called Antoine . . . Last night Felix told those students *The music comes first, not racking up linkis or gets, or booking fests, who knows how long fests will even last? Do what you need to do to get heard, but remember the music always comes first*—and they listened, three nodding heads, his students are in awe of him, worldwide DJ in their own neighborhood; little Hector even dresses like him, simple t-shirts and aviator shades.

Squinting now in the treeless sun, he lights up and draws, the smoke mellow as whiskey in his mouth: these pricey cigars arrived yesterday in a lacquered black humidor with a little note signed by Tom Hae, business partner, would-be wise man, *May our every vice enrich us.* Right now there are two, no, three unanswered pings from Tom Hae on the clip that shivers and purrs in the slash pocket of his robe—Felix gave him this robe, rough plum silk so dark it looks black, tailored cuffs and sash, he held it up, bemused, *Am I the kind of guy who wears something like this?* and *Well,* Felix said, *what kind of guy are you? You're my guy.*

This morning Felix was up and out early, filling the steam kettle, zipping the gym bag, while he rolled over into the warmth Felix left behind in bed, the smells of vetiver lotion and eucalyptus cold spray, the special scent of Felix's skin, then fell back to sleep, to dream—he dreams a lot these days, nights, threshold dreams of that unseen man and those long hallways, of empty dandelion fields under black sky dazzle, of bones and bricks and shit and buildings half-built or half-destroyed where parties rage under slippery silk banners and branches sing in the wind, sing till they snap—waking again and again to this apartment, this building that reminds him of the building he grew up in, the same low-rise street trees and slow commuter trains, though way more lux and with new window shields and red smart fences, last week the grid shivered and those fences went down, the weed boutique across the street got instantly robbed, the gourmet deli tagged with rubber spray paint, FUKKIN EAT ME!!! in angry pink.

At first this apartment felt like a haven: *Where's that, our place?* Felix asked him that before, Felix is constantly annoyed by New York but at ease here in a way he will never be, never was in that long-ago family apartment, or even his own industrial loft in the Factory days, the only place that ever felt like home to him was the Factory itself. Now the lease is coming due, and Felix wants, has been wanting, to settle somewhere, settle down, yet still he stalls, balks, why? Felix is his home, but his own center is something apart, *Ari's a maker, give him anything, anything at all—*

—like the aftertaste of last night's cocktails, and his own face glimpsed bluish and distorted on a doorside security screen, Sergey's footage of their wedding and the gold-trimmed saint cards Ava tucks into his bag, Angel Rafael and Holy Mother Mary, bodyguard Alonzo's waistband pistol and the empty bottle of Vismalux rolling on the Jump car's floor, the ice storms that killed Meghan's orchids

STATE OF NEW YORK

DEPARTMENT OF HEALTH

AFFIDAVIT, LICENSE and
CERTIFICATE OF
MARRIAGE

STATE FILE NUMBER
(THIS SPACE FOR STATE USE ONLY)

COUNTY _____
CITY/TOWN _____
DISTRICT NUMBER _____
REGISTER NUMBER _____

☐ SUPPLEMENTAL FILE

BRIDE/GROOM/SPOUSE	BRIDE/GROOM/SPOUSE
1. A. FULL NAME *ARI* *DANIEL* *REGON* FIRST — MIDDLE — CURRENT SURNAME	11. A. FULL NAME *FELIX* *RAFAEL* *PEREZ* FIRST — MIDDLE — CURRENT SURNAME
B. BIRTH NAME, IF DIFFERENT _____	B. BIRTH NAME, IF DIFFERENT _____
C. SURNAME AFTER MARRIAGE (OPTIONAL - SEE REVERSE) _____ D. SOCIAL SECURITY NUMBER ~~_____~~	C. SURNAME AFTER MARRIAGE (OPTIONAL - SEE REVERSE) _____ D. SOCIAL SECURITY NUMBER ~~_____~~
2. RESIDENCE A. *NEW YORK* B. *QUEENS* STATE — COUNTY	12. RESIDENCE A. *NEW YORK* B. *QUEENS* STATE — COUNTY
C. CHECK ONE AND SPECIFY CITY ☒ TOWN ☐ VILLAGE ☐	C. CHECK ONE AND SPECIFY CITY ☒ TOWN ☐ VILLAGE ☐
D. STREET ADDRESS ~~_____~~ ZIP ~~___~~	D. STREET ADDRESS ~~_____~~ ZIP ~~___~~
E. IS RESIDENCE WITHIN LIMITS OF CITY OR INCORPORATED VILLAGE? YES ☒ NO ☐	E. IS RESIDENCE WITHIN LIMITS OF CITY OR INCORPORATED VILLAGE? YES ☒ NO ☐
3. A. AGE *27* B. DATE OF BIRTH *07/4/92* C. SEX (OPTIONAL) *M* MM/DD/YYYY	13. A. AGE *25* B. DATE OF BIRTH *05/11/72* C. SEX (OPTIONAL) _____ MM/DD/YYYY
4. EMPLOYMENT A. USUAL OCCUPATION *PRODUCER* B. TYPE OF INDUSTRY OR BUSINESS *ENTERTAINMENT*	14. EMPLOYMENT A. USUAL OCCUPATION *MUSICIAN* B. TYPE OF INDUSTRY OR BUSINESS *ENTERTAINMENT*
5. PLACE OF BIRTH ~~_____~~ (CITY, STATE / COUNTRY, IF NOT USA)	15. PLACE OF BIRTH ~~_____~~ (CITY, STATE / COUNTRY, IF NOT USA)
6. FATHER OR PARENT A. NAME (OR MAIDEN NAME, IF APPLICABLE) *CALVIN REGON* B. COUNTRY OF BIRTH *USA*	16. FATHER OR PARENT A. NAME (OR MAIDEN NAME, IF APPLICABLE) *CARLOS PEREZ* B. COUNTRY OF BIRTH *DR*
7. MOTHER OR PARENT A. NAME (OR MAIDEN NAME, IF APPLICABLE) *SERAP DEMIR* B. COUNTRY OF BIRTH *TURKEY*	17. MOTHER OR PARENT A. NAME (OR MAIDEN NAME, IF APPLICABLE) *AVA MARIA GARCIA* B. COUNTRY OF BIRTH *USA*
8. NUMBER OF THIS MARRIAGE *1*	18. NUMBER OF THIS MARRIAGE *1*
9. PREVIOUS MARRIAGES A. NUMBER OF PREVIOUS MARRIAGES WHICH ENDED BY DIVORCE: _____ CIVIL ANNULMENT: _____ DEATH: _____	19. PREVIOUS MARRIAGES A. NUMBER OF PREVIOUS MARRIAGES WHICH ENDED BY DIVORCE: _____ CIVIL ANNULMENT: _____ DEATH: _____
B. HOW DID LAST MARRIAGE END? DIVORCE ☐ (A) ANNULMENT ☐ (B) DEATH ☐ (C)	B. HOW DID LAST MARRIAGE END? DIVORCE ☐ (A) ANNULMENT ☐ (B) DEATH ☐ (C)
C. DATE LAST MARRIAGE ENDED? _____ MM/DD/YYYY	C. DATE LAST MARRIAGE ENDED? _____ MM/DD/YYYY
D. ARE ANY FORMER SPOUSE(S) ALIVE? YES ☐ NO ☐	D. ARE ANY FORMER SPOUSE(S) ALIVE? YES ☐ NO ☐
10. IF PREVIOUSLY DIVORCED OR ANNULLED, PROVIDE THE FOLLOWING INFORMATION	20. IF PREVIOUSLY DIVORCED OR ANNULLED, PROVIDE THE FOLLOWING INFORMATION

	DATE OF DECREE (MONTH, DAY, YEAR)	PLACE ISSUED (CITY/COUNTY, STATE/COUNTRY, IF NOT USA)	AGAINST WHOM SELF	SPOUSE		DATE OF DECREE (MONTH, DAY, YEAR)	PLACE ISSUED (CITY/COUNTY, STATE/COUNTRY, IF NOT USA)	AGAINST WHOM SELF	SPOUSE
1ST			☐	☐	1ST			☐	☐
2ND			☐	☐	2ND			☐	☐
3RD			☐	☐	3RD			☐	☐
4TH			☐	☐	4TH			☐	☐

I duly swear/affirm, depose and say, that to the best of my knowledge and belief that the information I provided is true and that I declare that no legal impediment exists as to my right to enter into the marriage state.

21. SIGNATURE ▸ *[signature]*
 USE CURRENT NAME

22. SIGNATURE ▸ *[signature]*
 USE CURRENT NAME

23. SUBSCRIBED AND SWORN TO/AFFIRMED BEFORE ME
 SIGNATURE OF TOWN OR CITY CLERK ▸ _____ DATE _____

and the mud that buries Indigo Studio, the walled-off professionals on Argot and the art strays and true believers on Kerosene and the ruthless gossip mobs on Dive, the false calm of News Immediate and the doom screamers on Dayly, all telling him, showing him the same thing—that things end, change, break, amaze—everything operating in the spin that he no longer hunts or rides but lives inside, alert, aware, surviving—

—and he draws again, blows a pair of wavering smoke rings, then checks a new ping, a man's bare and gleaming ass, a flirty line of eyes, *DJ Boyz Boyz @ Tuesday Club wsg Valhalla!!* and *2nitez research let u know how it goez*, from Antwan, Antwan with the purple hair and thigh-slashed jeans, last night Antwan asked him a million business questions, leaning in close to ask them—

—as "Hey," from the balcony door, Felix in a cut-off NEVER-DAYS t-shirt and workout pants, tossing down his bag, "I waved at you, didn't you see me?" stepping out as Ari drops the clip back into his pocket, Felix's hand sliding past the robe's deep shawl collar to stroke his chest, his nipples and "You're too hot," Felix says. "Come on inside—"

—to lean against the cluttered kitchen island and kiss, breath of smoke, fresh sweat and sharp chlorine and "You smell like the gym," Ari says.

"You smell like bed," Felix says, tugging open the sash as Ari slides down Felix's shades, vintage and gold, Felix is smiling—

—then the door chime goes, three beats and the recognition tone, a voice, a woman's—"Bunny—" and "It's your girlfriend," Ari says; he slides the shades back up. "Did she follow you home?"

"I don't know why you do this—"

"I'm going to grab a shower."

"Ari, come on. She's only going to be here a minute, she's dropping something off—She already thinks you don't like her—"

"Why does she think of me at all," closing the bathroom door, clicking on the whirring filter fan but still he hears her enter, Bunny, Bunny Graves, her sharp bootheels, her seemingly friendly chat—"Alonzo said you had a great session this morning, Thomas is glad you can use his Sportshalle pass. Did Ari get the cigars Thomas sent?"—but he knows who really sent those cigars, and he knows she knows that, he dials the shower higher, he pictures her red relentless smile.

I SPREAD THE WHOLE EARTH OUT AS A MAP BEFORE ME. ON NO ONE SPOT OF ITS SURFACE COULD I PUT MY FINGER AND SAY, HERE IS SAFETY. —MARY WOLLSTONECRAFT SHELLEY

西半球

增訂萬國全圖

Warnung

Auszug aus der Ordnung für die Benutzung der M...

TWO

She could get a Jump or take the train, but she prefers to keep her feet under her, boots on the ground. People always ask *How can you walk in those things?* but she can run in heels and has, in the rain, on ice, up metal stairs, she can crack bottle glass or stomp a hole through chipboard. Thomas paid for these boots, his first purchase for her, not counting the *Eiskaffee* and the Zurich hotel room, when they got to Berlin he took her to a fetish bootmaker who measured her feet then asked what sort of heel she wanted, and smiled when she said *Railroad spikes*; these boots are the second-best thing Thomas ever gave her.

Ari Regon is the first.

Her trek today cuts through this humid, restless borough, rowhouses with potted plants looped to stoops with heavy wire, members-only cafés and smoke shops with doorway taser guards, charging kiosks ringed by skittish tourists, Green Circle health stations and vitamin smoothie stands, AV!TA !MMUN!TY! where a balding counter guy calls out as she passes, "Hey goddess, you feeling good?" dividing with her stride the other pedestrians as she heads for her noodle bar meeting with Ari's PA, Oona Dean. Oona's work handle is Unicorn16, and Unicorn16 is not easy to lure away from their protective workspace, but they believe this in-person meeting was specifically requested by Thomas on Ari's behalf; in fact Thomas knows nothing about it, Thomas is in another marathon session with Bergeron, working on their platform for "Mr. Perez," as Thomas insists on calling Felix in his acolytic way.

Felix is also working on that platform, a waste of time since if she does what she knows she can, it will never happen, but it means she can plausibly engineer spending time with him. Felix accepts her as a combination of Insomnious minder—like Alonzo the executive protection agent, former military, armed and watchful—and insider friend, always ready to chat, the way friends do; Felix never talks about his music, though she appreciates his extraordinary talent far better than Thomas ever could, but they talk about other people's music, other DJs he listens to—Elle Kay, Munkshood, 5 Mile Girl, Fuxury—along with everything else, how to sleep on planes, choose a good cabernet, *Go for the taste, never the cost,* art photographers and bare-knuckle boxing, Mary Wollstonecraft Shelley, the function of the corticofugal system—thanks to Agni's fucked-up upbringing she has been everywhere and has a headful of lore, whenever she pulls out some arcane fact Felix is amused and intrigued; sometimes their talks go long, Ari is so busy, Felix is so often alone.

And though fame has turned him wary, once he feels at ease Felix is very good company, thoughtful and funny and wry—and unassailably hot, wherever he goes people flirt, cruise, ask for linkis, every answer he gets is *yes.* At the couture vintage store the clerks kept bringing him shirts to try on, holding them close to his body, Felix did not ignore them so much as politely refuse to register their efforts, it made her laugh and *That happens to you a lot,* she said when they left the store, Alonzo a silent step behind. *Doesn't it.*

What? oh yeah, it used to be worse. I just wanted to show you, that's where Ari got me these shades. His wedding present to me—

Does Ari ever get tired of all that? Jealous?

He gave her a look she is still trying to configure, a rueful pride, a wistful roll of the eyes: *Ari? Ari doesn't get jealous.*

Never?

No.

Do you? but he did not take that bait, did he know it was bait?

because she already knows Felix gets jealous, she watches him watch Ari dance, and who he dances with, she sees that Felix needs Ari more than Ari needs Felix—

—and need and jealousy are tools, like self-doubt, and fear, and violence, she learned about those at the shrines, where the trucks stopped and turned off their lights; and from ZZ's long string of client stories; and first and worst from Agni, Agni's lies like the mirrors in her dressing room, this angle, that angle, *Everything depends on where you stand,* Agni said that, Agni said *Wouldn't it be safer to ask me for money than have sex with those turnpike men?* then when she asked laughed in her face, *Why would I give my money to a whore like you*—

—and up ahead is the checkerboard RAMEN BABY sign and its smiling baby logo, she is four minutes early but Unicorn16 is already there and waiting at a stand-up table, wearing a long-billed ballcap that shades their face and a Touch the Sky t-shirt. They start right in with spreadsheet talk and she pretends to listen, pretends to take notes while the bowls come and go, the noodles here are really very good, until "Is there a reason," says Unicorn16, carefully folding their napkin, "that Mr. Hae wanted us to talk live? and not on Crosschannel? That account's fully secure—"

"'I spread the whole earth out as a map before me. On no one spot of its surface could I put my finger and say, here is safety.'"

"What?"

"Thanks for taking the time," stepping away to pay the tab, learning just what she needed to learn, that next weekend's in-person meet will include Felix and Bergeron—Thomas is flying them to Wroclaw, to breathe each other's air or share electrons or something—but Ari will not be on that plane, Ari will stay behind, alone. Thomas does not know that, maybe even Felix does not, but Unicorn16 did, though Unicorn16 has no idea they shared that information, they were professional but guarded, they kept Ari's name out of the conversation. And that they could was the tell.

How to use that weekend, though, needs to be carefully planned.

Ari makes a point of avoiding her, not out of dislike, as Felix thinks—for all his street instincts, Felix is an innocent—but because Ari sees her as completely as she sees him. At first she thought she had to meet him right away, she almost asked Thomas to make that happen, but by the time Felix played at House of Hello, and Thomas asked her *Shall we go to New York?* she said *Not yet*—Thomas watched that show through a link instead, with Bergeron—because by then she knew better, knew not to go at Ari full-bore but from the sides, all sides, carving away everyone and everything else, then put herself in that empty place and say *Let's go.*

And that moment will be worth all the wait and the work, she saw that when they finally met, there in Insomnious's satellite office: on her feet between the blue-frosted windows and the rubber plant, watching Ari walk in, bespoke pinstripe vest and black diamond earrings, he barely shook her hand but when they touched he felt her, she knows he did because she felt him, a warm shock, electric as sex but not sex. And when he did not speak, would not, *I'm Bunny Graves,* she said. *And you're a great dancer.*

Is Bunny your real name?

Now she sees the Turkish takeaway café, right on her way like a nod from the universe if she believed in that shit. She asks the counter server twice "These are authentic?" and the server nods, "Oh yeah, my grandma, she loves our börek—" savory pastry, whiff of onion and potato packed in a red takeaway box, tucked carefully into her shoulderpack before she strides around one corner, then another, and at the third turn sees Felix heading up the street, Alonzo on his left. Neither of them see her—a failure on Alonzo's part, but not one she will report to Thomas—then Alonzo keys and checks the building's vestibule, Felix enters—

—as Ari stands above them all, in the sun, smoking, hair a mess, he does not see Felix, does not see her, will not acknowledge this box of pastries, the kind his mother might have made, the same way he did not acknowledge the cigars she carefully chose, or consent to meet her while Felix is gone; but they will meet all the same. The Rig Veda, Schopenhauer's notebooks, *Bitch Planet*, the twinkle of those little black diamonds, when she took his hand it was like looking at the stars when the constellations snap suddenly into view, this is the archer, this is the scorpion, this is the Golden Fleece. This is me. This is you. This is our world.

THREE

To call it a park would be stretching it, an irregular circle of grass between the chained-out dog park and the old smashball courts, but it does have a wooden bench, a charging pole and a water pump, and a half-dozen elm trees with half-budded yellow twigs, one tree so full of birds, grackles? starlings? that it seems to vibrate with their collective voice. Max sits on that bench, his bike parked behind, feeling the wind rise as he tilts his tablet, and enters the game that is his other home, *Birds of Paradise*—

—to see the purling white-capped waves, the shorebirds and narrow flying reptiles soaring over the concertina wire and the ever-rising ziggurat towers of skulls—all the deaths of this game end up there, bony white and socketed and still—and the paths lined with animate creeper vines, traveled by NPCs hidden or bold, the trees marked by messages and challenges and boasts, jokes and initials and sigils left by players, many of whom are still in-game. B of P fosters and rewards long-lasting player alliances, Clara insisted on that early on: players come to find and join a tribe in the squatter camps, or the forest, or the homesteads, or the biggest and most sought-after subsociety, a multistoried tugboat anchored just past the southern shore, where dragonboats float and fleets of manta rays and sharks patrol.

He has never been out there himself, his usage remains restricted: places he cannot visit, players he cannot see, though they see him; one player, Ajax, uses an avatar based on his own old myth, the sage who never leaves the game, spouting philosophy and ostenta-tiously writing in the air—embarrassing even to recall all that, *lux perpetua* does not come from him and it never did, why did he ever feel he needed to school the world? Mercifully Ajax is one of the players he cannot see, even the idea makes him queasy, triggering the migraine image of coding terrorist Jakka sliding and scurrying across the dunes, wearing his own deleted avatar like a harvested skin—that Clara still allowed him to come back here, play here, be here at all, is a kindness he can never repay, Clara trusted him but he trampled her trust, he deserved his deletion from this game.

Yet that deletion, that felt so terribly and authentically like a death—he wrote that to Ari the day it happened, **This is the nadir, this is nonbeing**—had paradoxically forced him from the prison he tried to build for himself, erased the dividing line between the physical and constructed worlds, and resolved for good his long sad duality of vision, making him fully, entirely, only who he is: onion-headed Zwiebel, present and responsive in both worlds without trying anymore to flee or master either. What did Ari say, before? *you're seeing real life like it's Y,* and he is—not the IR way, the way people do now with their Auras and Quirks, every momentary want or fear or monotony undercut or overlaid with a soothing or comic or stimulating personal vision, consciousness as insulated, curated cocoon—but the way Davide used to dream of, the many intersecting worlds within worlds within systems within patterns, a god's eye view, *curiosa felicitas . . .* Occasionally a seeker still finds him, looking to drill down into B of P's backstory, but *Clara Dix,* he always says, *Birds of Paradise is her game, ask her.* Whenever he sees Clara in-game, a three-armed, three-eyed traveler in a floppy DaVinci cap, he carefully keeps his distance, does Mathias still check up on them, on him? no way to be certain, but he means to shield Clara every way he can.

And he still writes down what he sees, everything he sees, a private history of the skulls, and the messages on the trees, the algae-green flotsam on Floatsam Beach, the black spots on the apples at Big Market Co-op, the neighborhood generator's kinked and veiny power lines, the God 4 the People squatters under their blue plastic banners to heaven and the fundie Jesus rioters outside the Groß

Moschee, the aggressive and proliferating security recruitment stands, *Citadel Keeps Your World Safer!* and the wars and rumors of wars, the leap and ebb of what no one calls culture anymore, what people play, watch, want, discard, destroy, all of it one rumbling jerking frieze of reality cycles, the dark transitions between transitional periods, the yugas that herald and hasten the biggest changes of all, the unstoppable ones that come like asteroids and blast to bedrock whatever civilization thinks it is, like lava on dry lichen—Canon, lore, apocrypha, why he writes any of it is a question he does not ask, what answer can matter until it is read?

Sometimes he thinks it must be for Ari, though they have not talked since that long-ago labyrinth call, marred by more of his own evasions, **Ari says you went dark on him** and he had, he hid. Yet if *the key point of the labyrinth is, you're lost until you're not,* why would Ari need any more notes from him? ever? Ari is not lost: guru strategist, impact consultant, talking mutable formats on a PlayOn gamecast, featured on New Future's *10 Essential Transmedial Creators*—Ari at number four behind an IR studio head and her actor husband, and a wunderkind Aura modder—interviewed by *Business Realities* beside the silent owner of Insomnious, Tom Hae like a human pillar of salt; Ari should be giving him notes, not the other way around, the way his own cry as he collapsed into darkness brought the quick sanity of Ari's response, he could almost see the smile behind it, **ok now just go play.**

Clara asked about Ari, the last time she came by his flat, bringing Weissbier and some swag from a deliberately retro quest game she and Simon are trying to shepherd into life, a black t-shirt and round black stickers with exploding golden letters, *CYCLOTRONICA!* Sitting at the wooden table, drinking as the Sunday sun went down, he asked her *How's it going?* and she shrugged, *Well, it's going! We're running some benchmarks, trying to optimize for this,* tapping her Quirk, *but shit's moving so fast, we're basically just trying to keep up . . . You hear much from Ari?*

Not for a while.

I heard the HERO build's pushed back again—dev team's got

a stranglehold NDA, but I thought Ari might have said something to you.

Pushed back why?

Nobody knows, but the take is there's trouble at the top, all that money flying around like shrapnel. Game Thief just did a big string about it, you see that?

No. I saw Garfman called it "a sinister cartoon."

My take, this is Mathias' final boss fuck you to Daedalus for firing him, you know how he loves to run a grudge. Look how he treated you! I'd hire you back in a minute if I could, you know that.

I know.

Eppur si muove, you're the only one who really gets it—Clara and her foundational theory of heliocentricity, before B of P was even a game, Clara believes in its power the way Galileo believed in the sun.

Then Clara opened another beer and asked, *How's it going for you?* and he said *Good,* because it is: he visits the game, he writes, rides his bike on long treks around the city, stocks shelves and makes deliveries for Big Market Co-op, meets from time to time for shoptalk and lagers with the coders. The flat's owners have moved on, but their subletting friends and colleagues come and go, for a month at a time, or a week; he is the one constant, in the smallest room with its uncurtained window and sturdy worktable and bed, he surprised himself by buying a new mattress for that bed, a firm mattress with a light hemp scent. A few times he and one of those coder friends have ended up on that mattress, but only for the weekend, or the night; he does not expect more, maybe does not even want more, being alone is not the same as being lonely.

Sometimes he sees Marfa's posts—she has finished her Factory interviews, Factory history, so no more MCSq2, now she is Marfa Carpenter, journo, helping her partner Pavel's precarious HIVE MIND apiary—and when he does see them, he feels less loss than a lingering warmth, there is no possible world where he and Marfa could have stayed together.

They have met for coffee a few times at the co-op, REDDY

ROASTERS is now THE PEOPLE'S CUP, the fresh baked muffins are gone but the scratched steel counter remains: the first time she was early and waiting, she brought a jar of Pavel's medicinal honey, she noted his new tattoo, a little blue onion beside the fading, screaming Tezcatlipoca, she asked to see his flat. But *You don't need to do wellness checks on me anymore,* he said, then squeezed her hand, the hand with the ouroboros ring, she squeezed back and said *Okay, point taken. The honey's good anyway.* The next time it was easier, she let him buy the coffee, she told him her news, *I'm working on another money ask for Pavel, "The Story Behind Hive Mind."*

He's still hurting for funding?

Hurting so hard I'd hit up Leon Cardenal—remember him?—if the fucker wasn't AWOL. But investors love stories. Like that doc thing Sergey Kendricks has going for Ari, Touch the Sky, *did I tell you I almost interviewed Sergey Kendricks? until he hid behind his NDA, even though it doesn't apply to me. I put him in touch with another shooter I interviewed, she was documenting the Factory freakosystem right before the building locked down.*

Before we went to see it, that time?

Way before. Anyway if this ask works, we'll be able to find a permanent place for the hives, or as permanent as shit gets nowadays.

And late last night, researching dance rituals, he stumbled on a post from long-ago Mila: her smile looks the same, brown hair braided back, in front of a brick storefront school, hand in hand with a man in black t-shirt and workout shorts, **Rashid & me, perfect partners!** And seeing Mila he felt a distant joy, a ripple from her final goodbye wave on the blue bike, there is no world where he and Mila could have stayed together either.

Now he takes a last quick survey of the beach—a party raft bobs up beside the tugboat; a neon octopus cruises the near shallows; a slim creature with woolly fur and a crest of blue feathers skims across the dunes, so gracefully that he pauses to watch and admire, not the first time he has seen that creature—But the wind beneath the park bench trees blows harder, the afternoon feels colder, so he stands, dusts the sand from his hands, logs out—

—to find the temp has definitely fallen, the birds are gone, the wind bends those yellow twigs below clouds merged into one angry charcoal line. As he unlocks his bike, someone calls out—"Hey!"—a young man, shaved head and baggy white parachute jacket, striding over, clearly angry, why? "Hey, you a delivery guy?"

"For Big Market. Why?"

"I'll tell you why! My last order had bugs in it. Bugs in the bread!"

"What kind of bugs?"

"I don't know, I'm not a fucking entomologist! Bugs! You better keep both eyes open—" and for emphasis kicks dirt at him, the dirt swirls, the white parachute sleeves blow back like wings as the young man storms away—

—and as he makes a quick note on his tablet, *bread bugs? weevils? locusts??* the first drops hit, insistent as hail, it is hail, little white stones thrown by the gods. Then the rain arrives, not in drops but a sudden gush, a torrent—

—and he shoves the tablet to his waterproof bag and drags on his anorak, to ride as fast as he can, half-blind and churning through that moving curtain of water—just like in B of P, the choice to stay or float away—jumping unseen curbs, skidding past floundering buses, until he reaches his place and its narrow porch overhang, to wring most of the drench on the doormat, then step inside to check if his tablet has survived; it has.

And on his screen a long blue feather curls and uncurls like a beckoning finger, a message bug from a player whose handle he does not recognize, *CHARMSKOOL*. He taps the feather twice, and the player's avatar hovers above, the slim woolly creature with the feathery crest, its eyes are intensely blue, its message asks *ZWIEBEL Q&A?*

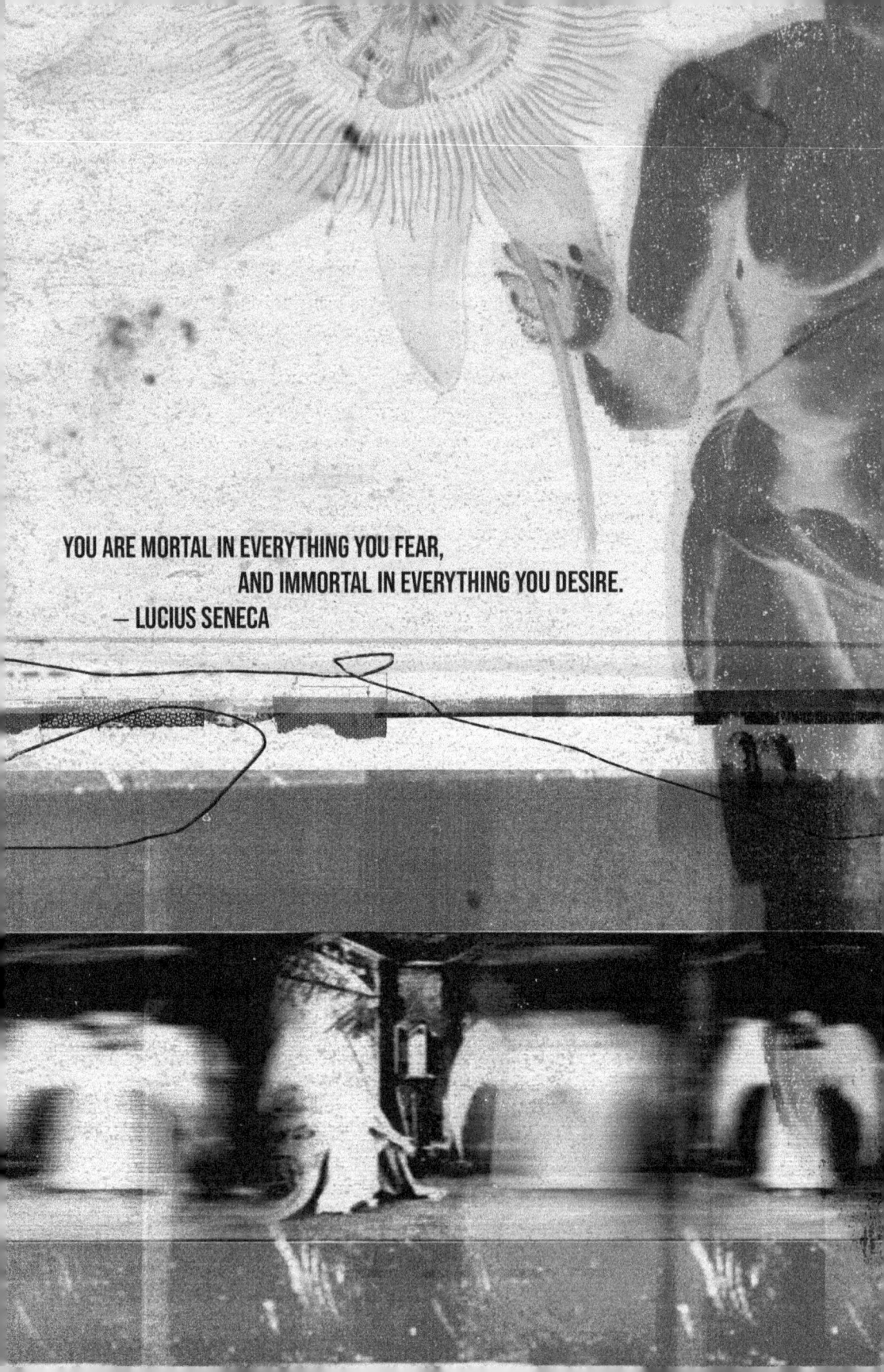

YOU ARE MORTAL IN EVERYTHING YOU FEAR,
AND IMMORTAL IN EVERYTHING YOU DESIRE.
— LUCIUS SENECA

FOUR

The elevator to the Insomnious office is quick, the doors hardly close before they open again: ninth floor, blue-frosted windows and a rubber plant that could be fake, Ari has never bothered to check, he never spends more time here than he has to, why does Tom Hae even pay for this dim satellite space? to make a place for him to go, an observable place? He knows someone is always watching.

The other offices on this floor are all third-tier financial, with nameplates like Indexx Capital and Fresh Battery, but the Insomnious door displays only the mountain graphic, black and gold: he remembers the old Insomnious tagline, WE NEVER SLEEP, he almost smiles. Coding himself in, he passes the receptionist's station—sometimes staffed and sometimes not, today it sits empty, a blank notepad on top and a cherry red shopping tote tucked beneath—and enters the main room, city-facing windows and a conference table where a blinking tablet sits waiting for him to thumbsign an agreement to lead a makers' retreat in Bonn. Tom Hae is urging him to do it, and Uni has already examined the terms, Uni says *nothing to turn blue over* but he has no intention of going to Bonn—or going on this weekend trip either, this morning he and Felix had another tussle about that, Felix still pressing him to change his mind. But he told Uni before *its not on my cal* and Uni pinged back a rare personal comment—

good call

??

Mr Hae's trip is not in your interests imo
u don't trust Hae 2 much do u

I work 4 u

—like the AWIP lawyers, Devon and Aliyah, when they combed wary through the Insomnious retainer, they told him *This structure is punitively complex. By design. Like a maze.*

Can you make it work?

If that's what you want. We work for you—

—and eventually he thumbsigned that retainer, took the title of chief belief officer at Insomnious, works on this still-unnamed platform—the prospectus defines it as *An experiential and repeatable entertainment enlightenment product,* Tom Hae's clunky definition, Tom Hae wants to call it after the Kabbalah or Carl Jung or some other favorite psych bible, while gamer Bergeron insists on calling it "Hero" after the in-tandem game; he keeps telling them both *It's not real without a real name,* though he has no name for it either—working days that turn to nights then back into days, wrangling budget bloat at amounts that once would have stunned him, along with build issues and personnel problems that Bergeron deflects or flat-out hides; he remembers Clara and her licorice-chewing team, he wants to talk directly to the devs—understanding less than half of what they do, he is learning, and they are willing—but Bergeron keeps stonewalling, *You have to respect the protocol, Regon!* the protocol? His protocol is to do what works.

So he keeps working, sometimes with Tom Hae and Bergeron, sometimes around them, sometimes he orders in a double espresso that he drinks alone while staring out the windows, an unlit cigar in his hand, wishing these windows would open so he could smoke: because every waking day five billion people tap in to play music and play games, and a platform with significant reach requires significant financials, and Bergeron and Tom Hae both believe in what Felix can do—while that black sun still rises over the golden mountain, *Transcendence Is Coming,* and when it does this platform will be ready: his platform. Felix said once *We're meant to make things together, things that last,* and when he makes this work Felix will play for the whole entangled world, every set, every beat, every note, every sound, a set that never ends; and he will dance.

Now he taps a note on the tablet, *declined/AR,* then checks the new pitches Uni sent on, from spinfluencers and marketing VPs who want him to boost a brand or pronounce on a project's worthiness; Uni declines almost all of them based on his noncompete, though the ones he can take, he sometimes does, for the fuck of it, the fun, like the Buck Rolls weed people who asked him to be their mascot, and the college dropout entrepreneurs with the talking sex toys, Felix said *Put that thing away, that thing never shuts up.* The chum-chasing sharks at Elden Golden & Pank offered a deal so fat he had to laugh, he showed that one to Tom Hae who smiled his thin smile: *Pank the poacher. I see he still has good taste.*

You know Alberto Pank?

Berto Pank went to Institut le Rosey. And I spent a few winters in Gstaad—

—and suddenly Elden Golden & Pank were dealing with a regulatory dirty bomb, Uni said it would pull serious fines, Uni made sure he saw that news. But when he brought it up to Tom Hae, Tom Hae's shrug was serene: *Cost of doing business, isn't it. Although connection is the only real currency now.*

Tom Hae likes to make statements like that—*Connection is the only real currency, belief is a consequence of ritual, expectation runs on predictive coding*—it reminds him of Jonas, Jonas said *The second time you smell saber-tooth tiger piss you run, that's predictive coding.* He used to think Tom Hae was a better-educated, better connected version of Jonas, but he knows now that Tom Hae is stranger than Jonas could ever be, and far more secretive, always that feeling of rooms within rooms, like the Y meet-up castle, and the Wroclaw trip's castle, maybe Tom Hae likes castles so he can have as many rooms as he needs.

He steps to the window's streaked and sunny view, checking the time—after this is lunch with Ava, he takes her out at least twice a month, sometimes with Felix, more often alone—as someone pings, is it Tom Hae? no, this is Antwan the student DJ, hands in prayer position, *Bonkers in Yonkers 2nite!! super want ur input!!!* with a prepaid top-tier ticket attached, even for a mid-level fest like this the VIP is pricey—

—as the outer door opens, footsteps quick and audible even on the carpet, without turning around he knows who it is so "If you're looking for Hae," he says, "he's not here."

"I know. Thomas is on his way to his rented chateau, on his rented plane."

He smells cherry hair pomade and a background street reek, like something wet or dead stuck to those fetish boots, he keeps staring out the window. "What does Hae think you're doing with Felix?"

"I have no idea. Entertaining him? I don't spend time with Felix because Thomas tells me to, I like Felix enormously—"

"Why do you talk to him about me?"

"Because you won't talk to me."

Finally he turns to look at her, red mouth, sleek white eyeliner, dark topknot hair and eyes even darker than Felix's, he has never felt energy like hers, like standing over a dancefloor sub, a sub in a club a million miles down. "Why didn't you go with them?"

"I didn't want to. Why didn't you?"

"Thanks for the cigars—"

—then out the door, one finger firm on DOWN, when the elevator door opens again he half-expects to see her waiting in the lobby, but only the security guard is there. And his clip pings again, how did Antwan get his number anyway? but then he smiles, because this is Felix—

Ready 2 leave
u said flt's @ 1? delayed?
I asked them 2 hold. Come with, baby
next time
Baby
ping when ur there

—adding a line of kisses, waiting for Felix to answer, waiting, but no answer comes.

Finally he exits, slipping on black Bellie sunglasses, the sun is all glare on this shadeless commercial block, its microbusinesses like feeder veins: a GLOBESHIP franchise, BREAKROOM WORK-OUT filled with people on treadmills, running and sweating and striving, an ANYTIME TEMPS kiosk where a bot tries to engage him, "Any job, anytime, twenty percent off today only—" while a skinny man in a greasy ballcap chugs along beside him, "Hey you want some, you know you want some!" some what? is the man a dealer? a beggar? but he shakes his head, when he reaches the subway steps the man falls back, is gone. Tom Hae likes to say *You can't shock a rat into seeing God,* but whose god? This city keeps on getting stranger.

Yet strange or not, he takes the trains instead of ExecuCars or even Jumps, conscious more and more of the ease and distance, the insulation, that a private car gives, or a third-floor balcony, or a threat screener like Alonzo—Alonzo is on that plane with Felix, for Felix he does not mind, but for himself . . . He used to go everywhere and do everything, until their bout of hard celebrity throttled back his freedom, so now is the time to look for it, to find it, on the street and in the world—

—and even on this subway platform, the security lights so stark and white that every grain of grit and splat of spit seems visible, half the people waiting look wired or annoyed, the other half are placidly wearing Auras or Quirks. A girl in a polka dot onesie is dancing, busking, to this week's banger, sing-shouting, "I wanna go—All the way, all the way—To you!" while two cute boys flank her, lip-syncing, are they part of her show or mocking her? No one else is paying any attention, but he gives her a nod of encouragement as the train arrives—

—and boarding, he tucks his new gold necklace inside his shirt, a coiling cobra necklace he bought on a whim, *BE AWARE! THIEVES ARE NEAR!* flashing red on the overhead screen. This car is freshly sprayed with disinfectant, its odor clogs his throat as he sways in the lurch and rumble, wedged beside a pair of women, one blank-eyed behind her Aura, the other muttering over a handful of red prayer beads, "Now and at the hour of our death—" and on the other side a man, a hot gym rat in skintight shorts who cruises him so shamelessly that even as he turns away he has to smile, nice to see someone who just wants to fuck, without calculating what Ari Regon can produce for him—

—though Ava does not at all approve of his train-riding, Ava in a flowery church blouse and gold earrings, passing him a KleenWipe when he rolls up to the little diner, her choice for their lunch date: "Use that, the trains are worse than ever! Viruses and crazy people, you can afford a car, take a car . . . You look very handsome today," as he bends to kiss her cheek. "Pio's at home?"

"Thank you," to her, to the server for the coffee, more chicory than coffee but he smiles anyway. "No, he just left. Work trip."

"Without you?" and when he nods, "Did that woman go, that Bunny?"

Surprised, more than surprised, "You met her?"

"Pio sent some pictures, and I thought, Oh, another girl like that Genie Hechman, at first I couldn't see what a girl like that would want with him. But Genie, poor thing, she was his friend," pausing for a sip of water, and he sips his own, remembering his onetime joke to Felix, *Genie would eat Suze in two bites*, but Bunny Graves would eat them both in one then spit them out, what does Bunny want with Felix anyway, what does she want from him? "Pio says this one's teaching him to play backgammon. Do you like her, Ri?"

"Felix likes her."

"I asked you," Ava's gaze suddenly demanding, so much like her son's that he smiles, puts his hand on hers on the tabletop and "I like what makes him happy," he says. "Just like you do."

"*You* make him happy. So stay off those trains! That actor got SARS-V on a train, it was a Jersey train but still. Did you see that? On Safe4U?"

"Safe4U is trash, don't look at that—"

"It was on Dayly too," turning her old-school phone to show him; on her screen is a picture of the three of them leaving some uptown restaurant, he and Ava side by side and talking, Felix on his other side, shades on, chin up, hand on his shoulder, Alonzo a blur behind. The journo who shot it sent it to Felix with a request for a lifestyle interview, *A look at FRegon's life beyond the decks*: Felix said no, then showed it to him, and he said *Send that to your mom, she'll love it*. And she did, she does, she loves it best when they are all together, *we're your family*.

Now this lunch ends with a hug at the curb, Ava shaking her finger at his cigar, shaking her head at their apartment, "I asked Pio if you were signing the lease again. It's a nice place, I'm not saying it's not nice, but you could live anywhere. Away from the city—"

"You live here—"

—as the black ExecuCar pulls up to drive her home, and three giggling girls approach him for linkis, "You're Buck, right? We love Buck Rolls, we want to be Buck Girls!" Then another ping, still not Felix, this is Sergey—

Meghan's @ gallery
u there 2
You know it

—which is the other reason he said no to Wroclaw: Sergey is in town to document Meg and Suze Duplantier, their shared installation at some legacy outpost in what used to be the gallery district, what started out as a short has turned into a full-length doc. Uni sent him an ArtEx interview of Suze talking nonstop about ritual and figuration, Lady Kidda and Beyoncé and someone called Pipi Rist, while Meg sat beside her, all in green, serene, until the interviewer asked about their project sponsors, listing names he did not know until one he did, Insomnious. And Meg's lips tightened at that name, so briefly it was easy to miss but he did not miss it, he wants to ask Meg why, an in-person ask, he messages back—

rollin

—and this time surrenders to ease and takes an ExecuCar himself, making one stop along the way, at a florist's, MIDNIGHT'S GARDEN over a black door, all the flowers in this narrow shop are white. And "What do you have," he asks the aproned clerk behind the counter, long hair bound up with green florist's wire, "that's like an orchid, but not an orchid?"

Turning to the shelves to choose a one-stalk bloom, deep green leaves and little curved petals, costly and frail and "It's actually called false orchid," the clerk says. "And it comes in this vintage jade cachepot—"

—that he carries carefully through the bending breeze into the car, then from the car to the gallery, where a scanner demands ENTER ID, he tries GUEST and the doors open. Inside are white walls lettered in red from concrete floor to ceiling, THE MAIDS OF ARTEMIS/SORIN + SUZE DU, and three huge and narrow freight crates, like coffins for giants. Behind one of those crates an assistant with a scanner argues with a stoic delivery agent, and behind another Sergey crouches, shooting, all in black, braids pulled back, and a new, impressive beard—

—and seeing Sergey all the memories rise, of *Touch the Sky,* everybody was watching them then, nonstop staring and thirsting and chasing, but nobody ever saw them the way Sergey did: saw them driven, joking, exhausted, under pressure and in love, saw Felix's anger and Meg's loneliness and his own bewilderment, Sergey always there beside them in that constant state of ambush, the hotel lobbies and VIP rooms and priority airport lounges, the blazing dark of Quest Fest and the neon embrace of House of Hello, Sergey still shooting from the curb as their Jump pulled away in the sunny morning after. And then all that warm strange daily intimacy was gone, all at once, like a closing eye—

—but now Sergey sees him again, Sergey smiles, they hug one-sided because of the flower and "Looking good," Ari says. "Like a, what's the word? Auteur?"

"You mean this?" tapping the new rig he wears, smaller even than the Piccolo, its silver lens discreet as expensive jewelry. "Or the beard?"

"Whenever Felix grows a beard, it means he's pissed off about something."

"Where is Felix?"

"On a plane. Where's Meg?"

"In there," nodding past the crates toward a glassed-in office. "Suze isn't here yet, so Meghan's stuck doing all the talking. You know how much she loves that—"

—as the office door opens and Meghan appears, dark green blazer and clip in hand, her sudden smile reflects his own—"Meg, hey—" and dissolves any distance between them, their diverging lives since she left AWIP and he and Felix moved here, dissolves too the time since they were last together, dancing between the pillars at House of Hello: that night she wore the orchid he sent, now she takes the little flower pot then hugs him hard and "Ari," she says. "Our mogul." Sergey shoots their reunion, while two people exit the office to watch, the gallery director whisper-ending a call, another assistant in a black-collared work shirt pointing a palmcam their way, Sergey briefly pivots to shoot back as "We'll step out," Meg says, "for a bite—"

—and Meg being Meghan, the place she has already chosen is just a few blocks away, an unmarked streetside door next to a medical spa, *Top Up Your Vax! 15-minute Detox Facials!* Two workers in smocks smoke twigarettes beside a sidewalk planter of yellowing ornamental grass, the smell like burning dirt follows them as they climb the long stairwell to a wee five-table café, where Sergey asks the server who is also apparently the owner, white shirt and silver sneakers, "Can we get some vodka? Cîroc, two shots?"

"I'll take Baraky," Ari says, "if you've got it."

"No alcohol. No liquor license, state's not selling them anymore," speaking only to Meghan, as if only Meghan is there. "But I've got a kickass saffron cordial, can I start you with that? And this is all on the house, it's an honor you're here. With the Maids—"

"I'm happy to be here, Ness, thank you. Suze and I both appreciate—"

"—because you know I follow the Maids, I follow *you!* We all do, we *feel* the Maids," palm to chest in a claiming gesture, and Ari sees Sergey shift slightly in his chair, the better to consider Ness:

Sergey shot hours and hours of those followers stalking Felix, he knows Sergey remembers those people too.

As they eat—a pale green celery consommé, a salad of thick-cut apricots and chopped beets, a sweating glass of mineral water for Ari, it tastes vaguely of salt—Sergey gives his news about *Touch the Sky*: "At first I thought I might need reshoots, remember I asked you? But I got everything. All that insanity, the ecstasy—Lisa, she's at Dissolve, the post house, Lisa keeps saying it's going to have big reach. She wants me to submit it to the IRL doc series," with a smile of pride and something else, Ari knows that feeling, the nervy rush before a make-or-break show, *here we go.* "And the trailer's giving heat already."

"Felix gets a lot of linkis from it."

"Fux too, Fux is getting booked all over, at the U-Turn party, and Soft Serve in Madrid—But they told me what they really want is to get into the studio, Indigo Studio, with Gussie Burns. They said no one gets it like Gussie Burns."

"Gus is blast. Suze probably doesn't think so, though," and when Meghan nods, Sergey looks mystified, so "They were a couple," Meghan explains. "Until Dark Park."

"I thought she was with the other guy, the label operator? Anyway Fux could do something wild for our doc," Sergey looking only at Meghan, as Ari hides his own smile, does Sergey know how his face changes when he looks at her? a completely different gaze, wide open, Sergey is clearly in love. "If I could just get her to listen to something besides those prehistoric flutes—"

"The Maenads danced to an aulos," Meghan says, "not a flute. But point taken. And Suze would prefer something more contemporary, too."

"'Contemporary,'" Sergey's visible lack of enthusiasm. "Like that tired motopop she listens to—Hold up," as his clip goes, the sound of whirring film. "Got to tap in, this is Lisa—"

And as Sergey turns from the table "The flower," Meghan says to Ari, "it's lovely, but I don't actually keep plants anymore. Since the conservatory."

"I saw. Nothing got saved?"

"In the old days, people tried to revive flowers from the cold with cinnamon," with a very small, very melancholy smile. "All those rare varieties! And my Stepney orchid—But it was freeing, in a way, losing things you love often is. I've sold my flat, I don't think you ever saw my flat—"

"Me and Felix were going to visit—"

"—and I'm staying with Suze, working in her studio, and in the fab shop, metal fabrication. It's been brilliant really. Grueling, but brilliant," with a smile, the window's sudden sunlight surrounds her like a halo, and he recalls how she came to him in the Indigo hallway, thrilled and shaken, smelling like smoke, saying *I understand what Suze calls the Artemis wilderness.* Now Suze is not her client but her collaborator, her name is first on that gallery wall, no more sieve or conduit for anyone, some seeds need fire to grow—

—and "It's time," he says. "It's your time, now."

"Our time," her gentle correction, "Suze works very hard. Almost as hard as you do . . . You look amazing, by the way. You must be happy."

"Working for Insomnious?" watching her lips tighten again at that name. "Why don't you like them? Is it Tom Hae?"

"'Like,'" shaking her head, a vast and tiny gesture. "There are VC firms that are loads worse on paper, some of the pitches I used to get for you and Felix—Criminal rubbish! And I'm not naïve, the money has to come from somewhere. But," dropping her voice, as if for secrecy, or warning, "there's a level of risk I find unacceptable."

"Risk how?"

"Risk of being compromised. Or subsumed. Suze feels differently, but—"

"Gallery says Suze just walked in," Sergey says, turning back to the table as Meghan's clip gives a series of little whistling drones, like bees dropping from the air, or bombs.

This time their pace is quicker, Meghan in the lead, Ari and Sergey behind, the breeze has died and the restless sky has lost its sun. And "Vondie Berenson," Sergey raising his voice while a siren whoops and chokes its way past, a red and black Citadel security van jerking to a stop down the block. "Vondie Berenson was shooting at Dark Factory, right around the time the building was sold. You know about that?"

"No," recalling his own last visit to the Factory, the air horns and singing, the laughter from high above, how many people were in the building that night? and Jonas outside in the sleazy sedan, *I worked for years, years!* Jonas who fired him then watched the Factory close, that night Jonas was already halfway to jail thanks to his "partners," those Sunset VC gangsters, is Jonas in jail still? Last time he checked, the Factory had been remade into a hotel, theme weekends and franchise DJs, a rooftop clubstaurant serving steak sticks and vials of vodka smoke, a joke. "Who's Vondie Berenson?"

"Doc shooter. Berenson and her wife were out shooting pilgrimage sites, holy sites. And since the Factory's where all this," nodding to him and to Meghan, "started, where Mister Minos started, her footage is really crucial. It could change people, like Felix changed me! And if you did the commentary—"

"Max should do that. Max Caspar, he's the one who—Look out," dodging a pair of delivery runners stopped dead on the sidewalk, one scowling up at an invisible address, the other staring in a scrolling fog through an Aura: not for the first time he wonders what Max thinks of those devices, Max would have a Quirk not an Aura, does Max use a Quirk? Does Max still talk to Marfa? "Was Marfa Carpenter the one who put you onto Berenson?"

"Yeah, looks like Carpenter talked to everybody. Even Felix! Everybody but you."

"I talked to her about Max. I talked to you about Max—"

"I remember. At those bleachers, before Quest Fest—"

"Max was in this even before Felix, Max is a big part of why everything happened. Why anything happened," and Max is the other reason he stayed off that plane, to put Sergey's wise and penetrating eye on Max's theories of xronos and kairos, *the same time* and that time feels like now, people outside *Birds of Paradise* need to hear Max too. "You can interview him in the game, right? I don't think he comes out much."

"That game where we met? And you asked me why I was a duck—"

"And you asked me why Felix was called Mister Minos—"

—as they turn the corner past a quick uprush of pigeons, pearl gray and palest pink, to see a gathered commotion outside the gallery, people in silver hardhats and lacy white dresses tattered dark at the hems, ten, a dozen, more. And when those people see Meghan they start shouting, reaching for her, pulling at her sleeves and her bag, pushing to follow her inside, while Sergey switches instantly to shooter mode, tracking her the same way he used to track Felix, that all-seeing, nimble backward dance—

—and past the doors, the sidewalk clamor closed out, Sergey pivots to catch Suze emerging from the director's office, Suze who still wears her biker's leathers, her long blonde hair sheared now into a spiky bob. And for Ari the sudden memory of cold concrete steps and paper plates of food, sitting with Suze outside Indigo as she showed him pictures of her studio, her white and static gods, *This is Artemis, mother of the hunt—*

—though Suze does not acknowledge him or glance toward Sergey, her focus is only on "Meghan! Meghan, look," holding up a cherry red shopping tote, pulling out a circlet of metal like barbed wire drenched in gold. Ari blinks, recognizing that tote, as "It's a gift," Suze says, "from Bunny Graves," while Meghan's smile of welcome stiffens and dies. "Bunny says only gold can crown a queen."

WE CAME INTO THIS WORLD SPITTIN' MAD,

RUNNIN' FULL BORE . . .

THE LORD PUT US HERE

TO PUNCH HOLES IN THE SKY.

—KELLY SUE DeCONNICK

FIVE

The gummy flowers are much too sweet, they stick to her teeth, she sucks at the gunk until "Fuck," spitting the whole greenish mess into the toilet, a few sticky drops falling onto the t-shirt she bought from a nomad bridge vendor, cheap white jersey and big gold letters, ARRIVED HAPPY LEFT NOT. She gave the rest of the gummies to the security guard who let her into this empty 4AM building, he thought he could play her, she told him *These are trip gummies, you'll be high as a kite by the time I come back down*—which was a lie, which was over an hour ago; and Thomas is still talking.

Thomas prefers to meet via video, but tonight, today, she insisted on audio, she does not want Thomas to know where she is—she knows where Thomas is, five hours ahead in the Hotel Monopol, sipping a teacup of warm water, the way he always starts his days— Thomas believes she is in the penthouse, he has no idea how much she hates that penthouse, its anxious blank luxury, its walk-in closets, the only time she ever goes there is to swap out clothes or have sex with Thomas when he comes to town, expand his dry appetite for abuse. But she will leave that penthouse behind when Ari and Felix leave the city—Thomas intends for them to leave, he even asked her to source the new location: *Somewhere out of the States would be best. Not China. Somewhere tranquil—*

What about Curaçao? Low pop density, and it's only underwater half the year.

Your sense of humor eludes me at times.

It always eludes you, but she did not say that, just as now she says nothing while Thomas goes on and on about his mystic sleepover with Felix and Dinky Kong Bergeron, not at the furnished chateau after all but in some boondocks building Felix found: "Mr. Perez's alternate setting worked out fairly well, the piano arrived not long after we did. Although Bergeron was a bit annoyed, I don't think he's used to roughing it," and Thomas makes a sound, a chuckle? She knows he thinks Bergeron is an idiot. "The space wasn't far from Baumpierre's atelier, you recall he hosted an event for me—"

"I do," lying, leaning against the cold sink console to look it up—Gerald Baumpierre, entertainment concierge for rich people with sky-high entitlement and no imagination, his company is called Terribly Keen—the sight of its tastefully cheeky logo calls up the memory of that party, another one of Thomas' liminal-industrial zones, she sat on a concrete ottoman and watched people drink pump-water cocktails and eat lamb brain mousse, someone asked her *Do you think this is what heaven is like?* and she said *You'll never know.* "I saw Felix played in the airport, too. He drew a crowd."

"Chopin Airport, yes, that public piano was barely in tune. But Mr. Perez made it through the Satie beautifully."

"He sure did," and she watched him do it on Kerosene while keeping her other eye on Dive, waiting for Ari to show up at the music fest with that little hustler Antwan Layne. And eventually there they were, Antwan stuck to Ari like a neon giveaway condom, igniting a feverish spurt of speculation and catcalling, the bulk of it on Dive—she sent dozens of those posts to Felix through a dozen masked accounts, *Regon has a fucktoi! hahaha boyz will b boyz, UGH NOT SEXXXY LIKE MINOS, dis ur man bro?!?*—what Thomas would call significant ROI on the cost of the VIP tickets.

Technically Thomas paid for those tickets, a miscellaneous expenditure like the funding for the Maids, when they were still called Maenads; does Ari know the myth of the Maenads and Dionysus? Another one of those nods from the universe . . . After her first sighting of Ari, spinning like a cyclotron on Thomas' screen, she ordered another bottle of wine and sat on the stiff white hotel bed to start her hunt, through endless linkis and posts from hero worshippers and would-be rivals, admiring colleagues and bitter frenemies, even

Ari's spa trainer ex and his left-behind father—Marfa Carpenter's interviews have been gold for that, locating the lost—while ignoring all the industry babble and parasocial thinkpieces, until as a kind of starter's gun she contacted Suze Duplantier—

—Suze who complained of being stymied by the art world, and snubbed by Felix—the same way he snubbed those vintage store clerks, and for the same reason, Suze's studio assistant Sébastien had a story to tell about that "Asterion" prototype, nude and horned and perfectly idealized—Suze left frustrated and adrift, until the Dark Park event threw her together with Meghan Sorin, Meghan Sorin who is Ari's longtime colleague and friend; Suze told her a lot of things, and she listened.

And then she commissioned the crown—a genius jeweler in Montreal, Sofia who used a 3D printer and what he called "lost wax method," ZZ would have adored him—and offered to broker the Maids' ongoing fabrication expenses, she likes the Maids, those big metal bitches, three meters tall and bulletproof, though she told Suze *Don't be too grateful, this is basically cocktail money for my investor. Is your partner happy with the deal?*

Bien sûr! I mean yes, of course—

Je parle français. Is Meghan Sorin your partner, are you two—

Partners in art, Suze's declaration meant to sound purely professional, but Suze is clearly hot for cool and reserved Meghan, just like that filmmaker Sergey Kendricks with his poker face and puppy dog eyes, Agni used to say *Don't bother believing what anyone tells you,* ZZ said *When I want to know what a client's really thinking, I look at their hands—*

"—and 'slain in the spirit,' all that nonsense, charismatics drooling and tithing, when it's actually a process of discernment. I keep advising Bergeron to read Taves and Asprem, but he prefers game reviews—Bunny? Are you there?"

"I'm here."

"Your voice sounds strange. Where are you?"

"In the bathroom," washing her face, the spidery white eyeliner residue, and refreshing her lipstick, Carna Purest Red, the only brand she ever uses; one of yesterday's tasks was to buy more, two thick new tubes, before going to the gallery where Suze was waiting, though Meghan was deliberately elsewhere, did Meghan learn that disappearing trick from Ari?

But she made good use of their separation, critiquing the sculptures' positioning, *Get them closer to the windows, no one's going to steal them,* then feeding Suze a story about those sidewalk true believers who call themselves Bridesmaids, how their passion points like an arrow to the intrinsic worth of Suze's art: the more she talked the more Suze nodded, until *Yes!* Suze said, *the myths as initiatory springboard, as energy reservoirs! I knew it instinctively.*

So we'll make sure the Bridesmaids have full access that night, which basically means two power switches and one system password, though the real hurdle will be observant and clever Meghan, who has seen unhinged fans in action before. *But Meghan should experience their appearance organically, the way it was at Dark Park. Don't you think?*

Dancing with her, under those trees—It was our moment.

Then we'll keep this between us, d'accord? because there needs to be chaos cooking at this opening, ready for Ari to enter, fresh from the fest and whatever fracture happens with Felix, chaos made for her to use—

—and now she crumples the paper washcloth, leaves the lav for the empty hallway with its twin EXIT signs, the overheads flashing on as she walks and falling away as she passes, let there be light, let there be dark, all the way to the Insomnious office, where she checks Ari's weekend Argot posts—a streamlined tumble of pulsing green lasers and smoke, various grinning DJs, festival boosters in multicolored lanyards, though no Antwan Layne—then watches Felix on Kerosene, hundreds of hearts and stars for his airport performance, the music so beautiful and sad, she looked it up, Erik Satie's *Gnossienne No. 1.* People stopped to listen, one then three then ten then half the travelers in the terminal, some were smiling, some closed their eyes and swayed, a few were crying, a hulking young guy in a kepi cap put his hand on Felix's shoulder then drew it back flustered when Felix turned around and smiled at him, that kepi cap guy would have followed Felix around the world for another chance at that smile—

"—an exceptionally discerning person, so I've arranged for you to test the game. One of Bergeron's staff will reach out to you, to set up a time—"

"No."

"What did you say?"

"I said no. I don't like games."

"Yet you play backgammon. With Mr. Perez . . . We can discuss. I expect to be in New York Tuesday, Tuesday evening at the latest, since—"

"Where's Felix?"

"—Mr. Perez has left for the airport—since the launch schedule has accelerated, proximity enables decision-making. Though I would have preferred Ari had been present," a lie, does Thomas know he is lying? Thomas was all agog to get his Mr. Perez alone, the same reason he tried to organize side trips for Ari, to Bonn and wherever else; Thomas has some peculiar feelings for Felix, not at all sexual, feelings that have everything to do with why this project even exists.

And backgammon—the only good thing she ever got from Agni— backgammon taught her how to assess not just her own moves, but the entire state of play, the possible and the actual, and do it very quickly. And her assessment here is that Thomas has been planning all this long before Ari, seeded by whatever hysterical epiphany Thomas thinks he experienced at Yale, and Felix's monster talent is the last and most essential component for Thomas to give in to those feelings, engineer this platform, deploy his performing god-catcher, and cut out his own heart—death is key to Thomas' plans, she can smell that craving a million miles away—then ascend to Valhalla or wherever, Thomas's concept of Heaven would be like playing Fuck Marry Kill with the devil and God—

"—the usual way, purely dialectical, and of course Bergeron believes 'viewing is doing.' But 'dvija,' the concept comes from Sanskrit, and that means—"

"I know what it means," digging with her tongue at a stray glob of gummy still stuck to one molar; her stomach aches with emptiness, with acid, she needs to eat something, then sleep while she can, things are going to start moving much faster now. "*Dvija* means 'twice-born,' born of the body and born of the rite. What did Ari say about what you all achieved?"

"He feels we've reached an important inflection point."

"'Now, at last, the Age of Desire.'"

"Your elliptical quotes!" which really means *Tell me who said that without me having to ask,* but she says only "You should read more fiction," which is funny because Thomas is sunk in his own fictions, and now is the time to free Ari before all this goes from theory to reality, to shit, the way things always do—

—the way it did at the shrine, beneath those black and shivering fir trees, as the naked man screamed, and the doors slammed on the sedan all the truck-fuckers used as a bullpen, they all ran away when they heard the *policja* sirens: but she stayed where she was till the *polijca* were gone and the man was gone, only the trees and the moon and the plastic Virgin Mary statue watched her crawl out past the weathered crosses and the dead dried snaky condoms, wipe her jenny knife and start walking, when she got far enough she pinged for a car and the driver took one startled look, *Ach, du heilige Scheiße, you get in a crash?*—

—and at the combat gym, instantly at ease with the sparring and the blows, but in rotation the other students avoided her, they complained to the instructors, *Basia never pulls her kicks, Basia's too rough!* until that midnight in the U-Bahn, a rare slippery misstep and she fell face-first down the steps, tasted filthy metal and her own blood, to hit bottom then jackknife back up—and see her boxing instructor on the platform opposite, staring at her, so she smiled at him to show she was okay, a big wide smile with bloody teeth. The next day that instructor took her aside to tell her the gym was refunding her membership, *The management feels this is not the right arena for your skills*—

—and at The Cellar and Eclipse and Lotus, all the dommes

avoided her except ZZ, ZZ said *It's not that they don't like you, they just can't figure you out!* ZZ never tried to figure her out, ZZ with her sweet eyes and ash blonde hair and fingers full of silver rings, ZZ shared lemon water and client stories in dungeon downtime—she thought the clients were hilarious, those lawyers and CFOs and corporate consultants, their panting greeds and shames, but ZZ had sympathy for them all—ZZ invited her for hibiscus tea in the sunny little flat, its windows crowded with climbing vines and fat succulents; and to eat tortilla soup at a floating restaurant, the boat rocked and the soup spilled and ZZ laughed; and to linger on the park's antique iron bridge, when she held ZZ's hand she felt those rings against her own skin, warmed by her clasp, ZZ asked only one question, *What should I call you?* and *Bunny,* she said, because ZZ loved rabbits, soft defenseless little escapees. *My name is Bunny . . .* Until *Miss Grób?* a woman in a gray wool pantsuit waiting for her outside the dungeon, Agni's minion because Agni had finally tracked her down, with a buy-out offer to *Legally separate yourself from the family,* the pantsuit woman said, *Mme Grób is offering generous terms* and *Here's my counteroffer,* she said, *tell Mme Grób I said to hurry up and die.* Then suddenly the landlady tripled the rent on the sunny little flat, the health department flagged out ZZ's sex work permit, ZZ cried in the dungeon hallway, *I can't understand why this is happening!* but she absolutely understood that angle of attack, she left the club and the city, left ZZ without even saying goodbye, went as fast as she could to draw the fire—

—and at the tired hospital's nearly-empty ICU, the wet and spotted sheets, the IVs feeding clear and bleeding cloudy, she hurried to take ZZ's limp and clammy hands, *Where are your rings? I'll get them back for you!* but it was already too late, ZZ curled in that bed, not peacefully arranged like a movie death, mouth open, eyes open, as if taking one last stunned look at the world. And she stood there shaking, shaking, gripping the personal effects bag, silver rings and cheap Bolero jeans and a jacket with a raveling collar, what had ZZ been doing, how had she been living, to dress like that, to get so ill? and *What happened to her!* she screamed at the ICU nurses, *what the fuck happened!* hearing one nurse say *Peritonitis, sepsis,* hearing another ask *You're a relative? How did you get in here?* feeling that nurse's pinky finger break, feeling the chemical ooze of the slip foam, the security guards sprayed it and fell but she ran, she threw the effects bag in the first trash bin she passed and kept on running, she ran all the way to Zurich and the tourists' leather bar, where Thomas sat sipping water, he asked her name and she told him a story ZZ told her, then another story—

"—still there? Bunny?"

"I'm here. But I have to go. I'll see you at the penthouse," tapping Thomas off, tapping up the music as loud as it will go, one of Felix's famous sets, the Jericho set where the other DJ passed out and the venue walls started to crack: and she leans shuddering against the glass, leans into those beats, their power and sheer control calming her, helping her breathe in and out—until she catches sight of her own reflection in the long windows, her hands, her fingers pinching at the scar on her forearm, a heart made of blood, not a Valentine's heart but the lump of meat that beats in the chest, a sacred heart carved with her jenny knife, she forces herself to stop—

—and go down to the lobby where there has been a shift change, this guard is older, with a company badge and a frown, he sets down his takeout cup but before he can speak "Where's the closest breakfast place?" she asks, and "There's a Sunnyside cart," he says, "over on the northwest corner. They got eggs, and wraps—Miss, this building's closed to visitors between two and five AM. How did you get in here?"

"I always get in. Have a nice morning—"

—and out into that morning as the dawn takes hold, in the smells of grease and scorched bread from the breakfast cart, some sourceless odor of ozone or bleach, and her own drying sweat, her boots in rhythm with Felix's beats, down this block that could be any block she ever walked, past the subway stairs that could lead to the MTA or the U-Bahn or the Métro, every city the same city, the same game played over and over in those offices, in sex clubs and bars, in private cars and private planes, and as she walks she pictures a domino series of falling walls, bricks falling onto bone, bone falling into dust because she and Ari are going to sweep this board clean, not because of trauma and not because of loss, but because ruin is the only thing that can end those games, all the endless games, *du heilige Scheiße,* a symphony for the wrecking crew.

THE WORLD HAD SEEN SO MANY AGES: THE AGE OF ENLIGHTENMENT;
OF REFORMATION; OF REASON. NOW, AT LAST, THE AGE OF DESIRE.
AND AFTER THIS, AN END TO AGES; AN END, PERHAPS, TO EVERYTHING.
—CLIVE BARKER

SIX

Almost midnight, but Big Market Co-op is lit up and busy, both shifts called in for a deep clean, more bugs in the bread, bugs everywhere. The manager is in their office, arguing with some distributor or supplier—"I *know* the price is stable, but if the goods are bad, what good is the price?"—as the bins and shelves are emptied and sprayed and wiped down, Max peering behind those bins for insects, finding only dust and occasional pebbles of mouse shit; still the feeling of life crawling just out of view persists.

He knows that feeling, feels it on all his deliveries, down streets where the sewers never seem to fully drain, the stink so pervasive that the brain just shuts it off, up wobbly back stairs and in elevators damp with roach paste, into apartment towers and shared flats and proto-squats that remind him of the Eastfield building before that whole ragged square got its brief commercial makeover. And everywhere he rides, swerving and gliding through this centerless city, everywhere he goes he knows that life is taking it all back, centimeter by centimeter, crawling things and creeping things, florid green and moldy gray and shimmering black, overgrowing, dying, clogging the conduits and splitting the bricks, uncontainable, ineradicable, just like the rot he used to ask for in B of P, the smell, the feel, the reality, here it all is. A part of him still fears what has to come next, the tsunami of collapse, but a larger part has given over all fear, recognizing it as the ego's last gasp while the water rises, no one can hold their breath for all eternity so until it happens, when it happens, all he has to do is ride his bike. And since he rides alone, leaving no one, going to no one, his own loss is lessened.

Now another driver appears, Lincoln with the street-modded racing bike, tonight Lincoln is wearing a coverall and gauntlets—like Pavel's beekeeper's suit, Marfa just sent him a video of Pavel tramping around behind some old gasoline station, the footpath marred with trash, Pavel murmuring *Well the bees don't ask for a lot of room but to give it to them, that's the best*—and "OK, everybody," Lincoln shouts, hefting a duct-taped homemade cannister. "This goes off in three, two, *one*—"

—igniting a shared rush for the alley, where Max halts halfway between the stacked piles of cardboard and the shipping pallets, to rub his eyes and open a can of warm Ever Tea, hoping this long day will shortly come to an end. Begun at six AM with another message from Clara, another step leading to the meeting with Mathias—Mathias wants something from him, and is using Clara to get it, like tongs touching roadkill—because Clara believes this meeting will relieve if not totally repair the enmity Mathias feels for him, and he owes Clara any help he can ever give—

—and now here she is again, determined and cheerful: "Max, hey, meet's finally a go!"

"I'm ready. When?"

"With Matty things are always now."

"I'm at work now. But that's okay—"

—setting down the tea to situate himself against those pallets, watch his tablet screen pop into a kaleidoscope of desert pink and teal, the colors swirling into an eye, that eye's pupil expanding—

—and there, staring back, is Mathias: no more referential avatars or flashy jade smiles, the joking game bro Matty B is long gone, this Mathias wears a jacket and black-rimmed glasses, a razor cut sheened with purple like a soured saint's halo. And before she blanks herself, Clara says, "Well you two have a lot to talk about, I'll let you get to it—"

—and at once Mathias starts talking, not to him but at him, about someone Mathias clearly dislikes, someone who "Never even played games, to him it's just process, 'repeating the cosmogonic act,' but what do bodhisattvas *really* do when shit goes sideways? They get the render times down!"

"I don't understand anything you just said."

"Why are you talking? Why aren't you listening?"

"I am listening."

"And I am talking, to you, Caspar, I can't believe I'm doing that but whatever—That 'chateau' he booked, that's not security, that's paranoia. Fake ascetic! He hated that other moldy place as much as I did! I could have set Minos up here, or anywhere. But Minos wanted that, or he said Minos did—"

"I still don't—"

"I'm getting to it!"

—and finally he begins to take in, if disjointedly, Mathias' real issue, a clandestine trip taken with Felix and Tom Hae, to someplace with poor ventilation and a piano, to settle philosophical differences, or problems, or something, over HERO, the core concept of which, according to Mathias, appears to be *find god, kill god, be god,* what could be more Matty B than that? But just as Clara said, there is trouble at the top: while Felix played the piano—"Don't misconstrue, Caspar, if Minos needs to play he should play—" it all collapsed into a circular battle between Mathias and Tom Hae, who Mathias says is failing the game, a failure somehow fatally tainted with echoes of Mathias' own ever-lamented *Fear of God,* and the endless colossal frustration that B of P did not lead to a total reboot of gaming itself: "Because gods *act* and gods *effect!* But whatever! Regon's the one who's going to make all this happen. Even though he blew off the trip—"

"Ari doesn't just blow things off. He must have had a reason."

"And that's the only reason I'm talking to you. You know him, so how much does Regon buy into this?" how much does Ari buy into what? the cosmogonic act? and when he does not immediately respond, Mathias shouts, "What's Regon going to do with HERO?"

"He's working on it with you. Shouldn't you already—"

"What *you* should do," Mathias enlarging his facial presence, big, bigger, like a balloon inflating itself, "what you *need* to do, is remember how you allowed a saboteur, a terrorist, to infiltrate B of P. I didn't press brand endangerment charges then, even though I could have. But I still can—"

"Oh wait now, wait," Clara suddenly appearing, she must have been backgrounding, Clara sounds calm but looks upset. "What happened with B of P has nothing to do with—"

"It has everything to do with it. They're both my games."

"B of P is my game too, Matty. You know how hard I worked, how I—"

"Dix, you were a dev cog, stand down. Caspar, find out what Regon's planning. And if either of you fails to delete this discussion immediately, you're both eternally fucked in this industry—"

—as the pupil contracts, the eye closes, a scrim or scum of white washes the colors away, and only Clara is there, mouth turned down at one corner like an angry comma, Clara is clearly furious so "It's okay," he says. "Clara, it's okay, I'll talk to Ari—"

"It's fuck-all to do with Ari! This is all about *him*—A dev cog! He never breaks anyone out! He stunts his techs, there's only one god in his machine—"

"He needs you more than you ever needed him. He even needs me—"

—remembering how he and Bergeron first met, the roly-poly Tezcat and anonymous Canary, Marfa brokered that for her own reasons but she had nothing to do with the instant, strange familiarity he felt, as if he could almost have been Mathias. Yet is this what he would have turned into? a talent stranded and dire, thrashing like a fish in a dry bucket? *Fear of God was supposed to clear the decks for enlightenment*, Mathias believed that, the way he believed B of P would open the gates to gamers' heaven, with its in-game MinosLAB culmination. But none of that happened, Ari said **this cant happen**, *what's Regon going to do with HERO*—

—and the alley doors slam suddenly wide on a sweet stench, the bug bomb's smoke, he breathes it in and coughs, coughs, while Clara says something inaudible, says it again, makes a frustrated can't-hear pantomime, then ends the call, amending a sad face and a skull face and a bright defiant thumbs-up. He ducks back inside, into the churn of the blower fans, past the manager yelling at Lincoln—"A fumigant, not a fog! That shit's on *everything* now!"—to scrabble up his bag and duck back out, still coughing, a fast ride home should clear this gunk from his throat—

—but as he rolls out of the fume zone, past the lager depot and the emergency clinic, a new notification arrives from B of P, a message bug, a gleaming beetle unfurling, *REGON SENT ME*—

—so he stops beneath one of the street trees, a tired yellow beech, to find waiting on the sunlit shore an adventurer avatar with strong stork wings, wide black eyes and "This is wild," the adventurer bird says. "Somebody really upped that grain—I'm Sergey Kendricks. Regon says we should talk."

"The filmmaker," and when the bird nods, "Ari sent me some of your stuff," clips from the Felix documentary, all the shine and violence, beats and tumbling bodies, all those faces reminding him of the high-piled skulls. "He said you were in here before."

"It looks a lot more real, now," the bird gazing around and up, up, at what? the drifting clouds, the constant rolling infinitude? and what would it be like, to see this world through a filmmaker's eye? Then Sergey Kendricks starts to describe another documentary, this one about the Factory's onsite denizens, the ones who came to investigate their own realities between the time Ari closed the doors and the sad new build-out Marfa took him once to see, Sergey Kendricks says "The commentary here is going to be essential, not just the backstory but the whole story. And Regon says you're the one who knows all about that."

"You see Ari a lot?"

"We had lunch last week."

"How's he doing?"

"He's Regon," fluttering one wing, the effect is akin to a smile. "So, you good with an interview? Should be an easy shoot, we can do it all in here, Regon says you don't like to leave—"

"No, I can leave. But there are much better people to talk to," thinking first of Clara, then of Marfa, both of whom would do a far better job: he glances away, into the shallows where the floating neon octopus pulses an inky purple, the effect half-shy, half-sly—

—and Sergey follows his glance, then suddenly stabs that sharp beak deep, its silver splash nowhere near the octopus or meant to be, but the octopus sucks itself up in alarm, darts away from them with one last shining pulse as "There's one for the nature doc," Sergey says. "You know, Regon was pretty strong that you were the one to do this. And Regon doesn't blow smoke."

"No, I know," because Ari does believe that he knows all about those inner meanings, the way Mathias believes he knows all about Ari, the way he used to believe he knew things too—*the empire of the senses, mycelium's not a human thing, ontologically it's all about patterns, if everything partakes of reality*—but all the layers have peeled away now, to show the vaster universe of everything he does *not* know, more and more every day, so "Thanks for the invitation," shaking his onion head. "But really, I can't do it."

"Think about it," dipping that beak again, "I'll check back . . . While I'm here, anything you think I should see?"

"The ziggurats, up there. The skulls."

Watching Sergey fly away, he wonders if he should message Ari now to explain his refusal, then ask Mathias' question, or at least tell Ari that Mathias is asking about him. But his body is still coughing beneath the sidewalk tree, coughing and yawning, in the co-op world there will need to be clean-up before there can be deliveries, his shift tomorrow will start painfully early—

—and "Hey," a soft hoarse determined voice, "hey Zwiebel—" and he turns, startled though somehow unsurprised to see again the woolly feathery creature, sparkling all over, approaching down the sand. "You got my feather. You didn't answer."

"I—No, sorry. You're Charmskool."

"On file, Charmian Duglass," a profile flashing briefly bright behind her, subclass and skills and history and build origin and pronouns, too much too fast for him to take in. And now he sees why Charmian sparkles, sees the dozens of miniscule totems woven into her pelt and dangling from her crest, all slowly and constantly revolving, like searchlights or miniature suns—little stars and spirals and moons and eyes and crosses, more than a few he does not recognize though one is definitely a pentagram, one looks like an Aztec jaguar skull, and one is the Zoroastrian farvahar—as if she is a universe unto herself, or an esoteric text made flesh. "So, the Q&A. Let's do that, Zwiebel."

"Now?" taking a half-step back, though a certain part of him, tired or not, wants to ask why she wears those symbols, clearly more than just decorations so who is Charmskool, Charmian, what is she about? But questions, more questions, why does everyone assume he has answers? so "It's pretty late," he says, "where I am. And tomorrow's a workday for me—"

"I'm working right now. On the pantheon. For the Yugacycle—"

"The what?"

"—and you're in it. First question: Are you familiar with Krishna, the god?"

Felix Perez Studio Notes

the motive for doing a thing is inevitably and ultimately ABOVE that thing - Sonny Rollins

a studio in Gowanus, Blaze said im crazy - the acoustics here are brutal but to play piano like this is like starting over, a cleanse. like teaching. teaching is clean.

make music out of music - Derrick May

panacousticon = everything is audible = geophony, biophony, cosmophony, anthropophony

the human body is open to sound in ways we have not even begun to grasp - Dr. Ibrahim Abra

Poulenc honored the sound of being human

Illy wants me to come back to indigo. Illy says people lived out in tents where i played, if i go back will they come back?

music comes from heaven, rites are shaped by earthly designs - Confucius = absorption proclivity, tellegen scales??? Tom Hae is a fucking weirdo, sometimes he scares me, like hes contagious

Mon Dieu, Mon Dieu, Que le Silence est Beau - Louise Bourgeois, written on musical notation sheet = ANAHATA, unstruck

music is vibration, vibration is a force, how can we know what that force IS, what if im not doing what it wants?? Mrs G took us once to hear a pipe organ blessed, the priest prayed "Awake O Sacred Instrument" and when the organist hit the pedals i got a rush up my back, pure heat, was going to tell Mrs G but then i didn't

really wanted to play in a church, that church in Barcelona thought the devil sent me or something, it depressed me a lot. music is holy!!! minosLAB was supposed to be my church but Ari knew that wouldn't work, Ari always knows

god i love him, i hear Ari more than anyone else

i hope hope fucking hope

SEVEN

"Watch your step," Felix says, holding open the rusting door for Ari to enter the rental studio's reception area, its ambient damp cut with the ghost of old cigarettes and fresh blunts, past a faded red security panel, *NOTICE/AVISO CAMERAS IN USE* and a table with a bright flutter of gig flyers and a pile of branded rave whistles, *Take 1 Make Noyz!!!* then head down a hallway, its line of anonymous roll-up doors like a U-Store-It, and into a windowless space that barely fits an upright piano and bench and an unfolded folding chair. A cat with a black and gold collar sleeps on that bench, and "His name is Goldie," Felix says. "He belongs to the dancers down the hall."

"Hey, Goldie," Ari bending to stroke the warm little body, the soft yellow fur. "You a studio cat? You like to dance?"

"We said we were going to adopt a cat, once."

"We still can."

"How?" sharp, scratching at his scruffy beard, that beard begun on the weekend trip and still unshaven. "A cat can't live in a carry-on. And this place—" letting the thought hang, turning away to gather the few personal objects the room contains: a steel travel mug and a half-bag of salted almonds, an old-school folder of paper sheet music, a cracked red glass candle, and a trio of books, *The Notebooks of Sonny Rollins, The Power of Music,* and one with a pink spiral on the cover, *Sound Waves and Healing—*

—as Ari considers this space, what has it really been for Felix? a bolthole where no one would look for him, the opposite of celebrity? a place to play alone? Felix has played no place else, booked no fests or gigs for FRegon since House of Hello, Felix is on hiatus like when they first met, *when I stopped playing*—yet not like that at all, Indigo is still in play, Felix says he means to record there again, has even posted about it on Kerosene—the only place Felix ever posts anything, the only feed he ever looks at—while Ilias tries hard not to push; last week some new headphones arrived, **Round Sound asked 4 u 2 beta these cans? maybe in studio??** and Felix answered **thanks Illy**, then set them aside for the students. No students ever came to this space, even he has never been here before, so why did Felix ask him to come here tonight? And why is Felix leaving it now?

But he says nothing, waiting, stroking purring Goldie, until "Where are we going?" Felix asks. "Some cocktail party?"

"Meg's pre-party. Her art show opening is tomorrow."

"Do I have to change my fucking shirt?"

"Not unless you want to," with a brief internal sigh: Felix has been like this ever since he got back, irritable, changeable, avoiding Ava, abrupt with Alonzo, at first he thought something must have happened on the trip but it seems like it was the trip itself: Felix said Tom Hae was nonstop full of jargon, faith frames and anomalous core experiences and Tellegen scales, *He said I was off the charts for absorption proclivity, what the fuck am I supposed to say to that? Giving me abstracts to read, articles, telling stories about when he was at Yale, quoting the Bible, "You shattered my deafness"*—And if Tom Hae was bad, Bergeron was worse, *Alonzo had to tell him to back off, he was in my face from the jump, "I totally respect you, I'd never ask you to do a private gig!" I'm thinking, Do they expect me to play, here? so I made them get a piano, and a place with decent acoustics—Where it was, this place I found, it wasn't too far from Indigo.*

Everything's far there.

Not that far. You know Gussie keeps asking when I'll be back, recounting how much work he had accomplished there, in the calm and quiet—Ari remembers that quiet, the depth of it, the crickets and the wind, the empty skies—and how it was *Past time to follow up Forking Paths, and I could teach there too.* Then swerving back to Tom Hae, *On Sunday night he wanted to drive three hours to some club in Wroclaw, I said if they were done working I was going home*—Wroclaw, the jitterbug accident, the dancing girlfriend, was that Bunny? so he asked *Was the club called Lecker?*

I think so, yeah. See, you know this stuff, you can talk to them. I never know what to say. I don't even know what they want from me—

What matters is what you want.

I wanted you to come with.

And that tension on departure is still between them, their closeness disrupted by a distance reunion has not solved: Felix so hungry for fucking the minute he got back, demanding it, demanding it early this morning as Alonzo waited downstairs, taking Ari from sleep with the force of his need, pulling off his workout pants and yanking down the sheets, rough hands and grinding and crying out *Baby, my baby!* but afterward not dozing or holding close, just watching him, why? what is Felix looking for, what does Felix think he sees? But he waits still, trusting that Felix will find a way to tell him, to say what the problem really is.

Now "The sound's not great," Felix says, "because of the wet," gently shifting Goldie down the bench, "but I wasn't really practicing. Otherwise I'd have been down here six hours a day."

"On this piano?"

"What should I have, a concert grand?" hands to the keys, a classical piece yet somehow fully outside time, a melancholy piece that keeps reaching for happiness, reaching and falling short. And Ari stands listening, feeling the way he always feels when Felix plays, the awe and the pride, and his own resolution, to give Felix the stage he deserves—But mid chord the music stops, Felix staring at the keys, asking, "Did you see me play, at the airport?"

"You know I did."

"They clapped at the end . . . I played it for you," half-turning on the bench, looking up as Ari bends down, to kiss, a kiss that holds all the tenderness these days have missed, and "I like when you play," Ari murmurs, and "I know," Felix whispers. "I know."

Then "It's getting time," Ari says, "we should get going," and Felix nods, and shutters the keyboard—

—as "There you are, bad boy!" a young woman's voice calling from the hallway, hot pink fade and Gunner Girlz t-shirt, while another young woman in white coveralls scoops Goldie close and pretends to scold: "You can't be hiding out at the neighbor's house! Sorry, Felix."

"It's fine, he's fine. Jae, Triana, this is my husband, this is Ari."

"Nice to meet. Your cat is cool."

"We found Goldie out by the canal," Jae says. "He's super independent! But he lives with us now, he's going with us to St. Paul."

"By the end of the month," Triana nods. "Are you guys still leaving the city too?"

And Ari looks to Felix, eyebrows up, but Felix gives Goldie a last pet—"Be good now, buddy—" then shoulders his bag and rolls down the metal door.

In the ExecuCar, Alonzo up front behind the partition, Felix positions himself at the half-open window to record the teeming traffic, the thumps and susurration of the bridge, as Ari leans back to check his feed—the News Immediate headlines, *Dubai aftershocks claim more lives, Scientists alarmed by raptor behavior, LaMid Pharma battles Grób Chemie takeover bid, Smart cup detonators spark terror hoax;* an escalating producers' spat on Argot tagging him to referee, he makes a comment to calm the heat without taking either side; a Felix tribute song on Kerosene, silly but heartfelt, he gives it a star, and two new dance challenges, in one he is a lion with a glitter mane, in the other a Franz France action hero with a bare muscled chest and strobing shades, the Franz France account gave that a star; all the usual fuckfests and jeering on Dive; a handful of new invitations he forwards to Uni—then in his thicket of pings a fresh one from Tom Hae, *You're heading to the art event with Mr. Perez?* although Tom Hae would already know that from Alonzo, Tom Hae is checking up on him again.

But where are they headed, really? *leaving the city,* to go where?

In all his plans he has none for where they will end up, their road to a future he used to fear would never appear, that fear is gone; yet where they should go, or should be, in this limbo time before the platform launches—Now Felix is looking at him, Felix his north star, so "We'll say hi to Meg," he says, "have a drink, then we'll go wherever you want. All right?" and finally Felix smiles, and takes his hand.

Still hand in hand they arrive at the party, Ari noting as he always does, as Felix refuses to do, the crowd's reaction—not everyone here knows who they are, but that they are known is clear, heads turn and appraising looks appear for the power couple, Felix in trainers and a worn-out Indigo t-shirt, Ari in head-to-toe Aswan black—as they enter this tenth floor office or workspace or whatever it used to be, this vacancy curated into someone's idea of an edgy industrial garden: drifts of paper leaves and spongy black rubber walkways, dwarf evergreens in trashcans dented to look old, a huge and flickering, writhing bonfire projection, and an iron arch roped with flowers, lurid red lilies like a thousand gaping mouths, where the gallery owner holds court with Meghan and Suze and a circle of well-wishers, Sergey shooting diligent beside.

But to Ari the whole space feels both unreal and too real, the décor so fake and tame yet rousing the memory of that night's very personal euphoria, the new tattooed stars still stinging on his wrist, the green flower blooming at his heart, and Felix all in white beneath the golden sparklers, playing on their first wedding day—till the twist and confusion of his fall, wrist wrenched as he hit the dirt, the spinning earth, like that event visual sent on by Bergeron's tech, what was her name? the whole world just a bubble in the endless dark, *Approved to use?*

And "This is part of Meghan's show?" Felix asks. "What's all this supposed to be?"

"It's supposed to be the yard at Indigo. Let's get a drink."

Glasses in hand—"Baraky? no? Bushmills? Any whiskey, then"— they separate, Felix retreating to stand beside the plyboard DJ booth, where a bored-looking DJ in a vintage Hï Ibiza jersey loops acceptable doom-fi beats: until the DJ notices Felix, stares at Felix, her beats begin to morph and quicken—

—while Ari takes his double whiskey into the crowd, drinking, roving, smiling but not engaging with the other guests—artists and culture climbers, the hangers-on that hang out at every party everywhere, clips up and gossiping—as he keeps moving toward that red arch, toward Meg in conversation now with someone in black cargo jeans who looks like a journo, when Meg sees him she smiles, makes a tiny beckoning wave—

—but Tom Hae is homing in, Bunny a step ahead, Tom Hae wearing a square-shouldered tobacco brown suit, a gleam in his smile, what room is Tom Hae in right now? as "Quite the turnout," Tom Hae says, "for your friend. You must be pleased Insomnious helped to fund this," raising a glass of something clear—

—so he returns the toast, the brassy whiskey's aftertaste like acetone, staring over his own glass at Bunny who has no drink to toast with, Bunny staring back, no one speaks until "I'll hope," Tom Hae says, "Mr. Perez is in good spirits tonight, and you two are free for a little dinner, after? Proximity enables decision-making—Edward, I didn't know you were in town," turning to receive another guest's fulsome greeting—

—as Ari leans closer to Bunny, close enough to smell that cherry pomade, close enough to ask, "Did you ever work at Lecker?"

"The domme club?" Her face changes, he has surprised her. "No, but I used to go there. Who told you that?"

My girlfriend and I were dancing at Lecker, I lost my footing, Tom Hae has a titanium ankle, is that down to her too, her assassin's boots? and "Why are you with him anyway?" his nod sideways to Tom Hae, still busy with the other guest. "You like his fancy suits?"

"You should see him naked," and despite himself Ari laughs. "That's a Bodley Pearce suit, I made him buy it just to be mean. That's how we met, he was looking for someone to be mean to him."

"For free?"

This time she laughs: Bunny definitely likes to spar, put strength to strength, he learned that from Uni's detailed précis—Uni started digging right after that fakeout side meet, Uni was *pissed*—they said *She must be using a serious scrubber* but Uni is serious too, they found those domme clubs and the hardcore boxing gym, the erratic travel and escalating assault misdemeanors, a patchwork of aggro and flight. And when he asked where Bunny gets her money, Uni said *She doesn't get it, she has it. Even though her family tries to pretend she doesn't exist,* because Bunny's real name is Basia Grób, from Grób Chemie the pharma company, she could buy Tom Hae—

—and "Would you do it for free?" with that red smile. "Money is power."

"Power is power—"

"Oh here's where the party is, here's the whole fucking party!" the loud ambush of a trio of boys, led by Antwan Layne in a tight black blazer, a professional look or at least more professional than the other boys' see-through vests and flashing nipple rings, Antwan crows "Ari!" and wraps him in an awkward, full-body hug, as if they are long-lost friends or brand-new lovers. "Ari, how's it vibing! And Bunny, hey Bunny—"

—as Bunny, Basia, takes one cold look at Antwan, then stalks off into the crowd, he watches her pass by the flower arch where Meg is watching her too, *a level of risk,* he and Meg have not talked since that lunch, but when he pinged her **wtf crown???** her answer was immediate and to the point: **You handle people superbly, you always have. Stay in charge.**

Now Antwan rallies from Basia's brushoff, boasting to his crew that "BIY was so blast, nobody could believe Ari was there! Ari, remember how Nanofesto couldn't believe it?" and he nods, he could hardly believe it himself, how strange it felt to be at a festival again, as if he had shown up to a teenage Blank Frank party, or like Felix's story of Wulf from Wafflesauce, *looking at my life from the outside, this lit-up little room.* To attend as a civilian, without a job to do, without Felix, felt even stranger, though it let him watch not just what happened but what drove its happening, all those hard-synced lanyards flashing acid yellow like caution signals no one stopped to read, all those aimless frantic bodies going back and forth like ants trapped in a glass, dancing, shoving, shouting, puking, way too many drink booths and too few first aid stations, and enough security for a venue twice the size, the red and black Citadel uniforms were everywhere.

All that night Antwan stayed close to him—when Nanofesto shook hands, *Wow, blast to meet, didn't know you'd be here!* and when Fretful and Dretful played a shoutout, *King Regon blessin us in the house tonight!* the follow spot as white and sudden as a bomb, he threw a V-for-vibe sign and the whole floor roared—and even closer in the elevated VIP lounge, a roped-off viewing platform tricked out with an inhalant bar and dwarf palm trees and blow-up sofas already sticky from spills, as servers circulated with trays of bliss bites and rum slushies, and couples kept ducking into the curtained "whirlpool booths," Antwan said *Those are hot!* but he rolled his eyes, he said *STD cocktail* and Antwan stared, then laughed as if he had made a joke.

Then Antwan asked *Do you have, like, a profile on Bisou?* Bisou the celebrity sex app, not a question Antwan should be asking: annoyed, he tapped his pinky ring, wedding ring, and *You don't need it anyway,* Antwan said, *everybody wants to get with you . . . You're on Argot, can you shoot me an invitation?* but he shook his head at that too, Argot is invitation-only for a reason, Antwan has less than no business there, and never through him. Still Antwan kept trying, *Well what about Dive, do you have a handle on Dive? Like a masked handle?*

I don't post on Dive.

But you look.

Everybody looks.

Still the questions continued, why were the BIY ticket prices tiered the way they were? who ran the backstage content for the festival stream? was it a bad idea to let fans upvote screen content? And because Antwan was Felix's student, and seemed to be trying to learn, enough to pay for two VIP passes, he stayed as patient as possible, he listened, he answered. Then when Antwan asked *Did*

Fretful and Dretful get booked because they blew up at Gigawatt? he asked the question back, *Would you have booked them? What would your line-up be?*

But Antwan's answer could have come straight from the old Pyramid posses, or any forgettable banger best-of: 200 BPM wall slammers, candyland DJs with cheap seat beats—Felix would be disappointed, Felix works so hard with these students, their nanobeat fads and god-tier anxieties, never charging for the classes, trying to help them hear the hum—so he asked *Didn't you listen to anything Felix played for you? Didn't you hear?*

FRegon, everything's easy for FRegon, he already has everything—*FRegon didn't teach us glitch promo, or journo interface, but coming up now, you need to go balloon-style, blow it up until it breaks! So I'd book myself first!*

And he considered Antwan—the ravenous ambition, the glassy striver's stare, how many times has he seen that stare? as if he is the keeper of whatever the striver wants most—and recalled himself as a boy younger than Antwan is now, living for parties, learning how to make things happen. One night he and that other Antoine bluffed their way into a swanky members-only bar, with a minimum spend that took their whole weekend's budget, and a mirrored lav where Antoine gave him a triumphant blowjob, just as they finished security caught them, and called the cappies on them for trespass: *Yes we'll press charges, this is a members' only club* as Antoine shouted back *One day Ari will run your stupid club!* And that memory made him smile, a smile Antwan seemed to take personally, Antwan moved even closer then, Antwan brushed his hand—

—so to put a stop to anything ridiculous, and remove himself entirely from Antwan's questions, he asked one of the VIP bouncers *Where's the green room?* a repurposed office meeting room, folding chairs and a tableful of liquor, smoke and laughter, players and producers, they were all glad to see him there, the bouncer closed the fire door on Antwan—

—and now one of the other boys is talking, at him not to him: "We asked what's Regon like. Know what Ant said?"

"'Relatable'!" shouts the third boy, as the theme from *Komedy Killers* drifts from his next-gen Aura.

"Ultra-relatable! Not like FHBG, driving that failure bus, FHBG is getting kicked off Weekend Ultra right now," the second boy staring through his own Aura as Ari mentally translates, Fucking Huge Big Guy the media ace, FHBG's name is actually Seth Smithson, he met Seth Smithson once at an industry lunch. And if Seth Smithson ever responded to shitclicks, if Seth Smithson walked in here right now, these boys would fawn all over him, distractible human bubbles floating from six-second banger ranks to lifetime feuds that last 24 hours, their attention so fickle it requires serious weight to hold it, at least Antwan can focus long enough to ask questions. Though Antwan should have taken all those questions to Felix—

—and he looks past the boys, through the crowd, trying to catch Felix's eye: but Felix is looking at Basia who stands beside him, Felix is frowning, the frown that means he is thinking hard about something that upsets him, *do you like her Ri, Felix likes her*—

—so "Enjoy the party," he says to the boys, then wades into the crowd, denser now, its voice one jittery wall-to-wall buzz like the background in a film, until suddenly "Regon!" from a voice he knows, Sergey's voice, Sergey now behind him. "Regon, hey, you see that shit?"

"Yeah, I saw," Sergey's string of pings about Max, how Max turned down the interview once and then again, Moon Man, meat man, the invisible man, who is Max now, the anti-guru? yet still as completely Max in those refusals as he ever was in his epic declarations, maybe even more so. But that Factory commentary has to happen, so "Make whatever plans you need," he says, "book the shoot through Uni if that helps. I'll make it work with Max—"

"What? No, not Max Caspar—outside, those Bridesmaids. You see *that*?"

"We came in through the back. What's going on?" But seeing now that Sergey is genuinely rattled—Sergey who stayed steady even at the heights of chaos, still shooting in the cherrypicker and the cappie van, the turmoil and screams—"Come on," he says, and steers Sergey to the bar then just behind it, a little square of seclusion screened by the portable icer and the stacked cases of bottles. The bartender gives them a look, he gives the bartender a tip, fat and in cash, "Double whiskey, we'll be out of here in a second," then again and more seriously to Sergey, "What's going on?"

"Look," Sergey lighting up his playback screen to show a crowd of people massed at this building's streetside entrance, the same silver hardhats and white skirts dragging the ground, but this group is twice the size of the one before, this group swarms that entrance, banging on the doors and "Cops foamed them out," Sergey says, "but they came right back, they must have used a polycutter to get through the smart fence. They tracked us over here, tracked *her*, they're always at the gallery now—"

"Gallery's got security?" remembering the sidewalk door that opened so obediently to GUEST.

"If you're stealing a painting, probably. For this? They'd have to hire it in."

"What does Meg say?"

"She says I'm overreacting. But she's seen how fast shit can go south, and so have you—"

—but now Felix is looking somewhere else, pointing at someone, who? as Basia nods, nods so "Meg's always on top of things," he says, distracted, "she knows—Hang on, I need to grab Felix—"

"From Bunny Graves," Sergey turning his camera their way, the red eye that looks at everything and is never surprised. "Bunny Graves hangs out at the gallery, too—"

—as he downs the double shot then skirts the crowd, calling "Felix! Felix, *hey*—" but the music drowns him out, jagged beats like a faltering heart, a man's voice moaning *Love it up, love it up!* and just as he reaches them, Basia steps away—

—and Felix takes his arm, hard, like the Genie wake at the papermill when Marko's goon tried to snatch him, the tattoo place when the squatters threw the riot, *Whatever happens don't let go,* Felix starts towing him toward the door but "Wait," he says, "Felix, wait—"

—and now the other guests are pointing their clips and watching, Tom Hae is watching, Basia has disappeared, the false fire flickers on the ceiling and the walls, the whiskey buzzes in his body, too much whiskey, he almost stumbles on that black unsteady path—

"—*wait*, we have to say something to Meg, good luck, something—"

"You think she needs luck?"

—as Antwan suddenly surfaces in the crowd, shouting "Ari! Ari, see you later!" throwing him the V-for-vibe sign, a gesture so bizarrely out of place that he almost laughs, automatically he gives it back—

—and "Gentlemen, this way," Alonzo just outside the door to shepherd them down the empty hallway, through double doors and a storage area stacked with unmarked boxes so clean they could be props, into a scuffed freight elevator and down to a delivery bay where an ExecuCar is already waiting, not the same sedan they used coming in but a gun-gray modified EUV. The door thunks shut behind them like a vault's enclosure, and "Reroute," Alonzo says to the car, then to them, "There was some trouble, street trouble, the police flagged it so I made the exit call. But we should be all right now, depending on itinerary. Where did you want to go?"

Ari looks to Felix, who has dropped his hand, sits head down in this cold car, shoulders hunched, closing in on himself, so "Give us a minute," Ari says; the partition goes up, the window goes dark, they sit in fraught and artificial silence until "You going to tell me," Ari says, "what the problem is?"

"You heard him. Street trouble."

"No, your problem. Ever since the trip, today, tonight—And what was she saying to you, before? What was B—"

"Just stop about Bunny!"

"You going to tell me where we're moving?"

"Were you ever going to tell me about your weekend? I saw you on Dive."

"Dive?" surprised. "You never go on Dive."

"Yeah," with a sideways look, half-accusing, half-unhappy, over what? "That BIY fest, why didn't you tell me you were going?"

"I wasn't planning to. But your kid bought me a ticket—"

"Antwan. Antwan was always bitching about how broke he was, guess he fixed that. Why didn't you tell me you went with him?"

"Because there's nothing to tell," exasperated now, Felix with his own secrets making everything around him into a secret too. "I saw some people, had some drinks, Nano said to say hi—"

"You had a night off and that's how you spent it? When you could have come with—"

"There was no reason for me to be in Wroclaw—"

"No *reason*—"

—as the partition opens an inch, two inches, Alonzo saying "Sorry, gentlemen, but we need to leave this garage. Do you know where you want to go?"

And Felix leans forward, past Ari, and "Nowhere," Felix says, staring straight ahead. "Home."

ZIPPER

FOMO because ENDO: Kiddo Despair is A Thing
by Penni Gorilla
@pennigee on Kerosene
@poisonpenni on Dive

ZIPPER gets mixed up a lot with an old-school fetish magazine with the same name and we are good with that! Confusion reigns! Nothing is what you think it is! And that's what a lot of The Kiddos are feeling now, mass confusion, doom, ache, sense of loss, so sad. At Juggernaut Fest I asked some kiddos WHAT'S UR PROB?

. . . Antwan Layne is a kiddo with DJ dreemz who drops names like other DJs drop beats. Antwan says: *I just did a chiptrack launch that was totally influenced by Ari Regon. I vibed so hard with Ari at BIY, everybody was watching us! Working with him is my dream and I just want to do that because you need somebody to blow you up, that's how FRegon [Mister Minos] got where he is. But shit is always moving with you or without you, shit will pass you right by.*

EIGHT

The gallery's windows are still covered by safety boards, the RES-
TORATION 212 logo is orange and bullseye-bright. And "Look,"
Suze says, pointing out the fresh silver scrawls across those boards,
white wedding white wedding bridesmaids BANG ON. "After all that,
they came back . . . Vandals."

Inside is dim, *THE MAIDS OF ARTEMIS* lettering is gone,
the silver paint painted over and the debris swept away, the gallery
director's office light is on but that door is firmly closed. The Maids
stand swathed in heavy movers' canvas, she tugs at the corner of one
tarp but "No one can touch them," Suze says, Suze who smells like
desperation and hotel soap, with her dirty hair and stained white
shirt Suze could almost pass for a Bridesmaid herself. "The police
have finished, but the insurance company is sending another asses-
sor, they can't be touched or moved until—Bunny, *please* don't—"

"I paid for them," still tugging, the tarp will not come free so she
reaches from beneath, like touching a corpse under a sheet: shreds
of fabric still snagged on the sharp edges, dried paint smeared there
too, and blood, blood will leave pits in stainless steel . . . The door
ID and alarms were turned off, she did that herself, but in the end
it never mattered, the opening barely started before the Bridesmaids
overran the door, how many? thirty? fifty? and more in the street,
they smashed the windows and sprayed paint on everything—on
her too, she had to throw her clothes away, cleaned her boots twice
but the shine is still there—those human maenads trampling the
social order with their bare feet, drunk on violence and screaming
for *ekstasis*, all that was missing was the music as they passed the

crown from hand to hand, stripped naked and climbed the Maids, a few fell, a few got cut, one got stuck and nearly severed her arm.

And she stood just inside the gallery director's office, watching it all—the crown's savage glitter in the overheads, the shower of blood and flung dresses, the fleeing shit-scared guests, the gallery director's panic as the Bridesmaids pushed her down and crushed her clip underfoot—watching and waiting for Ari to show up for his good friend Meghan, she messaged Felix twice but Felix did not answer, she waited but Ari never came—

"—on Dive they're tagging me 'Suicide Suze,' my Eyeball account is still frozen, what gallery will ever show me now? *Tout est ruiné—*"

—the same thing Suze said, screamed, at Sergey, *Tout est ruiné! Why the fuck are you still shooting?* but Sergey kept on, silent, dogged, his hands visibly shaking. And when the gallery had been secured by the shockbots and cops, and the paramedics had come and gone, the real battle started, Meghan cornering Suze between two of the Maids, not loud but quiet, absolute ice: *How did this happen, Suze? Who let them in?*

I never—

Who let them in?

Meghan, I never thought—

What we made is over. And that girl is terribly hurt—Turn that off, icy too to Sergey who was unbelievably still filming, he did as she said but then tried, surprisingly, to defend Suze: *Hold up, this can't be all on Suze. She wasn't at Quest Fest with us, she doesn't know how bad it can get,* but Meghan said *You weren't at Dark Park,* and Sergey flinched, as if she had hurt him. *But you did warn me. And I never should have agreed to involve Insomnious, and Bunny Graves—*

—so she exited that office, crunching through the scattered glass, not like entering Armageddon after all but like stepping into a reality show, she walked straight up to Meghan and *Climb down off the cross,* she said. *Nobody died.*

Do not, do not attempt to have an opinion on this tragedy—

I have lots of opinions. On lots of tragedies, staring at Meghan who stared back until finally looking away, walking away, trailed by silent Sergey, as Suze stood in the mess and cried.

And now Suze is crying again, "Meghan won't answer me, that fucking Sergey knows where she is but he won't tell me! Bunny, what are we going to *do*?"

"Shut up," dropping the corner of the tarp, this Maid no nexus for power anymore, not a metal queen or her sisters either, just a trio of objects, insured commercial items on a list: and that makes her angry, because Suze got the name right the first time, these were meant to be Maenads, but all Suze really wanted was a successful career reboot and an attractive industry-adjacent girlfriend. Which was why she took back the crown from that melee—it sits in her travel bag, wrapped in a mushroom leather vest—with Ari she could have put that crown to real use, she and Ari could have detonated that fucking crown so "You deserve everything you got," she says, "you don't play with gods and not get played yourself. And if you do get any insurance money, you should give it to that one-armed girl, *she* understands. Don't contact me again—"

—and she gives the bullseye board a sideways kick before slamming back into the ExecuCar, pushing aside her ripstop travel bag, giving the car her destination address, "Expedite arrival," to Ari and Felix's place—

—though not their place for much longer, Ari put a buy hold on a new place, a square little building with a square little courtyard, where it rains sideways and the gravel road leads nowhere but to Indigo Studio. She heard that news from Felix the morning after the opening, Felix sent a real estate link and ten seconds of happy piano music, **look where we're going!** though she had a list of potential rentals all ready to show, places Thomas had approved, but Ari's PA beat her to it, one point for Unicorn Oona . . . Thomas believes this is sheer defiance on Ari's part, Thomas told her so just an hour ago, after their final penthouse fuck in those Porthault sheets with the navy blue print like a detailed diagram of a headache, she tossed down the bit gag and Thomas rubbed his mouth, sat up and said,

This relocation, its timing, especially its destination—All negative impacts. Deliberately negative.

You wanted them to move, well, they're moving.

I told you to source the next site.

I made the list, you saw it. But Ari picked that place.

Ari Regon is a partner in this venture, not its principal—

Ari Regon is your chief belief officer, and he's married to your human tuning fork. Face it, Thomas, you've got a tiger by the tail, and the tiger does whatever the tiger wants to do.

And his stare narrowed and furrowed, became ugly—*It's a serious mistake for anyone to underestimate my tenacity in this venture. Including you, Bunny*—so she shoved him back down and straddled him, a serious combat move, she locked her thighs and immobilized his white unready flesh, she knew she was hurting him, she squeezed even harder and *Your tiger is restless,* she said. *You better hang on.*

And then she packed, everything she needs into the travel bag—the wrapped crown and mushroom jeans that match the vest, the bridge vendor's t-shirt, a hoodie she got at Schiphol, a parachute silk ballgown, the backgammon board—everything else left behind in that mausoleum walk-in, all the rest of the clothes she brought here, bought here, the lingerie Thomas gave her that she never wore, she walked out wearing this black Vertrauen jacket and the workout pants with reinforced knees that she took from the boxing gym, ready, now, to follow Ari and Felix, not as Thomas' adjunct but as herself, covert, overt, however she can work it, however she can get herself installed with them in Nowheresville.

But why did Ari choose that town? so close to the old studio, it must be for Felix—tapping up another of his sets, and "Volume," she says to the car, "volume, volume," until the bass shakes her shoulders and spine, throat and thighs: this is the music she always wanted to hear, even better than the hardcore battle chants she used to play to wind herself up for a match, this is music that makes things happen . . . She had asked Felix, finally, about the Jericho set, as they sat in late afternoon shadow on some restaurant's walled-in patio, over the dregs of a salad niçoise and shaobing bread and a bottle of overpriced Riesling. At first he was quiet, then *What was it like?* he said. *The whole place was moving, I was making it move, the people, walls, all of it. I wasn't even wearing the mask that time,* the Mister Minos face, does Felix still have that, is it lost somewhere or trashed? *And they never wanted me to stop, Alaine didn't want me to stop—*

Then why did you?

I had to.

Why did you have to?

I couldn't handle it then, picking up the bottle, refilling their glasses. *Let's finish this off.*

But that opened him, finally, to talk about his music, how he studies the power of polyphony, acoustic ecology and *musique concrète,* the subtle body and the autonomic nervous system and the way sound releases dopamine and serotonin, how certain frequencies can change perception, change behavior, simulate the effects of nitrous oxide and regulate vascular function, and *There's this surgeon,* he said, *Dr. Ibrahim Abra, he uses music in the ER instead of anesthesia.*

And his twin sister is a tournament backgammon player. Razia Abra.

Seriously? you know her? Did you ever play her?

No. I never played tournaments, only money games.

What's a money game?

I'll show you sometime.

Only now there is no more time, Ari is in a hurry, so "Expedite," she says, and the car accelerates, past rowhouses and bodegas, people queueing, walking, hurrying, even stressed and diminished this is still a real city, Ari and Felix have never lived in a place like the place they will live in now. But she knows exactly what it will be like there, a shitty town with a shitty language no one speaks, bad roads and iffy grid access, at least two overpriced state liquor shops and a very old church with a Virgin on top, like the towns around the shrine—

"Message incoming," the car says, overriding the music.

"Display only," and on the display is some Insomnious lackey revoking all her logins and clearances, insisting she leave the Exe-cuCar immediately, are they going to send a chase car to run her down? so "Delete," she says. "And expedite. And volume—"

"Caution! Caution!" the car braking hard enough to jostle her, stopped by an accident just ahead, a Rite Now bot tangled up with a bike, a woman crying in the street beside a smashed bag of red sauce and fat pink chunks like someone's guts. Other cars honk, a trash truck bleats, and she watches, impatient, about to get out and walk—until she sees a man hurrying from the curb to help the woman, waving over a pair of gawkers to help too, she sees it is Alonzo. And when the car restarts and reroutes to their building, she sees Alonzo on the corner, they both arrive at the door at the same time, he gives her his usual professional smile: "Miss Graves. Good afternoon."

"Good afternoon, Alonzo." His shirt is spotted with red sauce, it looks like blood. "Busy day?"

"Mr. Perez is with the movers," pointing to the black and white box truck parked at the service door, UNITED RELOCATION. "Mr. Regon is out."

"Are you looking forward to relocating?"

"I'll let Mr. Perez know you're here."

Upstairs, she angles around a pair of those movers as they jockey a bed frame down the hallway, past a line of waiting items—café chairs, a tall industrial lamp, a cheap globe lamp in a blow-up carton—while inside another mover zipbags piles of pillows and sheets, is it Ari or Felix who likes to sleep on mulberry silk? She examines that growing emptiness, alert in the way an animal must feel in another animal's den: she and Felix have rarely met here, and she has never seen Ari here at all, but his things are here, a German espresso grinder, a gaudy green glass ashtray and the black humidor she sent, a black jacket on the back of the sofa, it looks like the jacket she has on; and Felix's things too, a pair of bright blue hand weights, three audio travel cases with cables coiled and piled beside, the kitchen island's bottles of whiskey and the California cabernet she knows Felix likes, and a small bouquet of blush roses in a silver vase, the roses not fully fresh, petals tinged and curved with brown; their life is here. And suddenly her heart hurts, a suckerpunch memory of ZZ's little flat, the plants and sun and teacups full of deep red tea, what happened to those teacups, did someone throw them away? She should have kept ZZ's rings, at least one of her rings—

—as "No, the sofa stays, but the—Bunny, hey, hi," Felix emerging past the movers, energized and beautiful: no more frayed t-shirt, his beard is shaved and his hair cut short, the new cut shows off his cheekbones and the flower tattooed behind his ear, but there are shadows under his eyes—

—and she knows why, she put them there, she keeps Felix fixated every way she can, always asking where Ari is, making sure the event DJ played "Love It Up" to remind Felix of Julian Zero, another interloper out to steal his man, making sure Antwan did what she told him to do, stir the shit, fawn and flirt, give that stupid V-for-vibe sign that she has successfully recast to Felix as a private joke between Ari and Antwan—

—though Antwan threw her a curve with his brainless greeting, so once Ari and Felix had gone she tracked Antwan to the lav, where he stood adjusting his blazer in the mirror, he looked like a valet parking attendant. With one hand she drove him against that glass, with the other she pinned him there and said, *I told you to pretend you don't know me, why didn't you do what I told you?*

I didn't mean—I'm sorry! I'm sorry! I just forgot, Ari's so hot, I just want him in my mouth—

I don't care where you want him, keep your loose mouth shut, smelling the fear on Antwan like sweating metal, finally she let him go; Antwan's use is over. What she needs now is to find a way, make a way, to stay beside them, keep feeding that jealousy till Felix finally breaks—

—and now Felix is smiling at her—"I'll miss our hangouts—"

and she smiles back, feeling a strange dismay, like watching a car bearing down on a little animal in the road, driving that car, knowing she will not swerve, knowing there is no other way; Felix really is an innocent, the way ZZ was an innocent, and she does like him enormously, she did not lie to Ari, she has no intention of ever lying to Ari. Yet Ari carried Felix from street fests to a fame so steep they had to leap to leave it behind, she knows when she takes Ari it will break Felix's heart, but will it harm his talent too? his music? Permanently?

Still smiling, she balances the backgammon board on the sofa, the last place left to sit—Agni's vintage Vuitton board, ebony and black, Agni taught her to play on this board, maybe Agni is still looking for it—and "A quick game," she says. "For the road."

"I really thought," Felix rolling high, moving first, "that I'd be better at this by now. But you still beat my ass every time."

"Any beginner can beat any grand master, it depends on the checkers and the luck," watching the way his hands move on the board, hesitant, considering, so different from his hands on the decks. "On my way here I went past that gallery, it's still a shitshow. You must be glad you didn't go."

"Those Bridesmaid people—I told him it wasn't safe and I was right."

The blood, the dancing, the paint, the screams. "Safe, no, but at least their motivation was pure. Like your fans."

"'Pure'?" with a frown, it makes him look older. "Like the five million jackoff linkis I used to get from those antler bros? Or the Twistie fuck shots people made with me in them? that my *husband* saw, Ari had to see those all the time! Or the flower people, always running up on us after shows, and at restaurants, we had to stop going to restaurants, stop going anywhere. One time they got me alone in a hotel elevator and shoved flowers in my face, down my shirt, my pants—"

"What about the ones who danced?"

"That's not the same thing. These people only wanted to get onto me. Onto us—"

"Maybe they needed you."

"Needing what you do and needing you, two different things. You don't know what it's like to be chased."

And her own frown—"You don't think so—" how long has she been running? from Agni and the apartment in Arles, and those punishing family trips, trips engineered to prove to her there was nothing to want but what she already had, not art or god or the ancient earth, not sex or poetry, Agni caught her reading Sylvia Plath so Agni made her stand over Sylvia Plath's grave, *Sylvia Plath stuck her head in a gas oven*, while her own mother gave up and died in that apartment, Agni broke her mother, Agni will never, ever break her. "You don't know where I come from."

"I'm pretty sure you come from money," making a move that surprises her, an offensive move that puts one of her checkers on the bar and out of play. "This new place, things are going to change for us there. And it's not far from where we got married," with a sweet and sudden smile. "We've never had a real home, I want us to have that, have a cat—Where's your home, anyway? When you're not doing this."

Doing this is my home, but she does not say that, instead "I didn't know you were a cat daddy!" and he laughs: "Oh, Ari likes cats too. He liked Goldie."

"Where is Ari?"

Rolling his eyes: "One more goodbye lunch with my mom," Ava Perez, all that firepower of maternal love, nothing she has ever had but Felix takes it all for granted. "She loves Ari—"

"Everybody loves Ari."

"—but she's cool with us moving, she never understood why we stayed here anyway. I mean, I grew up here," with a shrug, that quintessential New Yorker shrug. "And Ari can roll anywhere. I did like teaching at Beat Shack though, I liked my students—"

"Even Antwan Layne?"

"Not so much," rubbing his chin, that nervous tell, does Felix know he does it, is that what the beard is about? "But he never missed a class."

"He probably took your class just to meet Ari. Ugh, the garbage people post—"

—as Felix's clip goes, a soft staccato like a glass heart beating, a voice saying *Meet me, meet me,* Ari's voice, she turns toward the door just as "Hey," Ari entering, Felix rising, the checkers tilting useless from their positions, their game is over. "Look what Ava gave me," holding out two little cards. "For safe travels."

"Gave us," Felix taking the cards from him, little gold-edged prayer cards, turning them so she can see too and "I know this guy," Felix says, a burly man shouldering a calm chubby baby across a rushing river. "St. Christopher, he's the patron saint of travelers. But this one—"

—a shining frame around the dark unyielding face, its prominent red scars, the narrow infant held like a trophy, not one of the mild Virgins at the shrines, this is an ikon of war and "That's the Black Madonna," she says. "She works miracles."

"Good to know," Ari says, as Felix loops an arm around him, white bracelet bright against Ari's black-striped scarf and "That's real bone," she says, "isn't it," knowing it is, and "It's for good luck," Felix says. "He gave it to me, a long time ago."

"And you gave him that," pointing to the necklace Ari wears, as gold as the Maenad crown, a shot in the dark but a lucky shot because "No," Felix says, "actually I didn't. Who gave you that?"

But Ari does not answer, slips instead from Felix's hold to root around in the glassware mess of the kitchen island, and "Lost my lighter," he says with a little frown. "Maybe the movers will find it—I told them they could finish up without us. You almost ready?"

"Been ready," and unsmiling Felix heads into the hallway, his voice louder than it needs to be: "All the audio stuff, that's special handling. Make sure it's marked that way—"

—as she takes up those cards, thinking fast, fast, the way she would with the board spread out before her, the checkers and the luck and "Well, safe travels," she says to Ari. "It's not that far, but it's very different there, places like that have a real learning curve—"

"I learned something on my way here—you just got fired. How did that happen?"

Fired, Thomas would frame it that way, as if she was just another Insomnious employee, she should have squeezed Thomas till he screamed. "Thomas is unhappy, mostly with you. He needed someone to blame."

"Hae's not too happy with Alonzo either, Alonzo's getting fired as soon as we leave."

"Alonzo?" Unknown terrain *and* a brand-new bodyguard? what a stupid move for Thomas to make. "What for?"

"Bullshit reason. It's a long story." He takes two cigars from the humidor, then smiles at her, what kind of smile is that? like humor but not, irresistible, unnerving, is he pissed off, is he about to laugh? "Hae's going to put some new security on us, so I'm thinking we should have some of our own. What do you think, Basia Grób? You want to dance?"

ONLY GOLD CAN CROWN A QUEEN   —BUNNY GRAVES

nine

"RPG yeah," Charmi says, ticking off the list in the air, feather by feather appearing, touching the water, floating away. "FPS not a lot. Puzzle games yeah. And story games are the best, narrative develops all your skills," nodding to Max who nods back, perched across from her on this minimalist raft, her choice of venue for their talks, a triangle of sticks and wriggling vines floating out where the horizon glows gold and ocher, rocking on the constant swells; he has never been this far out before. "And your skills are who you are."

"Are they?"

"Yes," decisively. "In *Tomorrowville* it was strength. *Asmodeus 2* was mimicry and composure, *Valhalla* was resource management, *Khartoum Devils* was scribe skills, *Blight Maniacs* was persistence," one hand up to tally those qualities: whenever she moves, all the symbols in her pelt quicken, the crosses and spirals, a staring eye staring at him now like the eyes of the meat-pink sharks swimming beside the raft, opening and closing their giant circular mouths, like ragged funnels filled with teeth. "I never played to beat a game, I played for skills."

"You played a lot of games," and many more than he has, a humbling array; he is privately pleased that she approves of B of P's design, and what she calls its post-doom culture. "A lot different from the ones I played, coming up."

"Yes. You played *Monomania*—From, wait, from Sunk Cost Media," in the precise tone she uses when she is consulting her Quirk, the in-game and outside Charmi in rare visual communication, Charmi seeks always to get it right. "That's ironic."

"Yeah. Not too popular."

"It didn't last very long. And you played *Knights of the Crystal, Winter Wolves, Human Eclipse, BurnOut,* those old classic games—Why are you smiling?"

And he shrugs as he smiles, how to explain his pleasure in following the fleet switchback pathways of her thoughts, as if they play a game within this game, a game only she understands . . . In one way Charmi reminds him of Marfa, the way she sifted and dug to find him, Charmi will keep digging until she hits paydirt, no matter how arduous or far. But unlike Marfa, Charmi is not spring-loaded and single-tracked, she is multiplicitous and bewildering: one minute blunt and focused, another detached and tutorial, another riding a stratospheric cloud of theory, she contains multitudes, and all those multitudes are Charmi.

He has never viewed her in-game profile, or looked up her MePage, would Charmi even have a MePage? or tried to learn what she does as Charmian Duglass, what other games she plays, what she reads besides philosophy, where she lives: he knows almost nothing about her, not even if her eyes are as intensely blue in real life, or even blue at all.

To be included in her project has been a mystifying privilege, her Yugacycle so formidable in its complexity, its theories and references cross-indexed and as far-reaching as mycelium, history, archaeology, mythology, ludology, Charmi says *We don't ride the yuga cycles, they ride us. That's a joke. Sort of.* Because each yuga, each age—gold, silver, bronze, iron—forcibly creates a complete overhaul of material and intellectual worlds, while between the yugas come the times of pure collapse, *Transitional periods, like things are now. Chain typhoons, civil wars, viruses—*

That new one in Chengdu, the hyperpyrexia one, I read some people were spiking fevers at 105, 106 degrees.

44 Celsius, it's not survivable. And the crop shortages, the citrus failures—

We can't even get the hydro ones anymore at the co-op.

Co-op?

Big Market Co-op. Where I work.

Oh. I didn't know you worked at a grocery market.

Yet Charmi is cheerful, a true scholar pleased to make connections as she maps the great impending end: *Games teach us that users can break any system. And decay is ultimately generative. Loam. Fecundity. Change, "change passes through all things without exception," and every myth system has a rubric for change, just like every cycle has its contemporary avatars. I'm still looking for the Kali, but as soon as I found you, I found the Shiva too. I had a couple other potentials, but they were wrong.*

Shiva?

His name is Ari Regon—

What?

—and even though it's from a competing mythos, Felix Perez is Asterion, Minotaurus—the mask he's famous for, that level of self-ID is really determinant. That's another aspect of the Iron Yuga, magical thinking. It's a sociogenic phenomenon, it feeds belief, and belief drives behavior—

—yet does Charmi truly believe, does she give this cycle theory the same real-world credence as food shortages and killer fevers? Her breadth of knowledge would serve a Yale classicist—the "skool" in "Charmskool" may be literal, she could be a professor, a mythologist, or only (only! is he still a Kunstfarm snob?) a gifted maverick savant—so as a serious scholar the myth is, has to be, entirely theoretical for her.

Yet hearing her name those avatars startled him, a sharp, almost frightened *frisson*: he never told her about his own conflation of Ari with dancing Shiva. And Krishna . . . Self-identification, magical thinking, a guy with a sky-blue head.

But he has not asked, the same way he has not asked about the possible duration of their interview, each talk they have checks off another box for her, but how many boxes are there? how much time? The more time they spend together—as he hurries through or shunts off his daily chores, eats his quick meals at the co-op, rearranges his delivery schedule to stay in-game as much as he can, his manager is increasingly irked but he pointed out with total truth that *I'm never late for shifts, and I never brought in a homemade stink bomb,* so for now he gets the changes he requests—the more time he wants to spend together, talking together, talking about things other than the game; about her. But his own awkwardness hobbles him, how to do that? as a response to one of her questions? as a sidebar? just start? And worse even than the awkwardness is the worry, what if his questions seem intrusive to her, what if she turns away from the interview? from him?

He does not want Charmi to turn away from him.

Now "These beasts," she says mildly, "too rude," as the sharks surround them again, nudging the raft, rocking it like bullies on a school bus—until she slaps hard at the water, a slap that makes a ripple that makes a wave that sends those sharks spinning, whirl-pooling away as the raft rocks and tilts, nearly capsizing: he holds on tight like a scared kid on a rollercoaster, he has never died in here and has no idea what would happen if he did, all he knows for sure is his life bar can never fully recharge, there is some stamina drain but he has no idea how to find it, let alone fix it.

But Charmi calmly rides that rocking, though her totems blink crazily, like neon signs fighting to sync themselves, and says, as if there is no disruption, "So why did you play, then? If not for skills?"

"I played," easing his grip as the water starts to calm, "to be in a different world. To get away."

"What do you mean, 'get away'? Get away from what?"

"From—" should he say it? this talk is not meant to be about his personal woes, especially the ones he left behind, but she is asking, and it is true—"From myself. Like in *Monomania,* there's this one level, the Introverse, I'd play my way there, then stay there," completely alone in that manufactured void, all spatial awareness of eyes and hands dissolving, the longer he stayed the less himself he was, the less he was anyone, like an underwater diver at the most extreme depths, floating past the need to breathe, suspended in serenity . . . He played here that way too, in the beta days, walking into this water that then was purely darkness, until he glimpsed the faraway sparkle of unknown creatures, bottom dwellers unhindered by any pressure; he used to get headaches from that, Davide called it "rapture of the deep" but he knows now it was the precursor to that punishing migraine blindness, yet another kind of darkness; and another kind still on the roof of Dark Factory, as he stood cold beyond shivering, composed as a corpse and staring into the sunrise, and afterward hunched in the squat, still perfectly cold, to ask Ari *Do you know Krishna? The universe in Krishna's mouth?*

And eerily, "Krishna opened his mouth," Charmi says, "to show the universe inside him, 'I am the origin of all those things that are about to be.' That's from the Gita. The original Sanskrit is best, but it's sometimes hard to tell when the story stops and the religion starts. Do you have a favorite translation?"

"Uh, no. Not yet."

"I thought you might prefer the Kosinski. 'Some games are played by entities who need to test a theory. Entities with many potential players can always play again.'"

"What?"

"'If the world ends, does that mean it's over? The gods have to live somewhere. So does everything else.'"

"That's from the Kosinski?"

"That's from you," pointing a finger, its totem a minuscule shining moon. "Players came here to ask you questions, then compiled what you said. There are full-thread Maxism archives on Kerosene, and four—wait, five—*Birds of Paradise* spirituality groups on Korridor, the tag is Max Wisdom. That's how I found you."

Max Wisdom? with an inner squirm of sheer embarrassment, that he once took himself so seriously, that Charmi should find it out—And then he laughs, a quick cleansing burst, and "I'm glad somebody made something useful out of anything I said. And I'm glad you found me. Really glad."

Yet she does not answer or respond, there is only silence, just the rhythmic voice of the waves, was that the wrong thing for him to say? how wrong? so to quickly say something else "Look," he says, and points to those waves, where the funnel sharks are arrowing back, a fast determined V. "Here they come again."

Charmi kneels—"Hang on—" leaning so far out it seems she must falter, fall into the water that churns with the sharks' arrival, but she does not falter, she reaches past the lead shark's shiny dorsal fin, into empty air, and "Hang *on*," again, emphatic, directive, he sees she means hang onto her so he does, arms around her waist, the first time he has touched her—

—and somehow they ride the sharks' momentum, plowing their way across the waves, scattering and swamping the other rafts, swerving past the bigger crafts and the tugboat as the players onboard watch them and cheer, to slew rapid into shore in a sweeping sideways fantail of foam and flying sand—

—and Charmi laughs, a hoarse delighted laugh: "Turbo, so turbo! Thanks for the ride, Zambi!" who is she talking to? then "This is Zwiebel, another Z," looking to him, waiting, until he understands, he says, "Sorry. I can't interact with Zambi, I can't see them."

"Oh. You have interblocks, wait, by choice?"

"Not my choice. My usage is formally restricted."

"Oh. *Oh*—"

"It's okay, it's not a big deal—"

"It is a big deal. I should have known," with such obvious distress that he feels bad himself, she is focused on one part of his history, not every part of it, especially the redacted parts, so "We can talk about it sometime," he says, "if you want. But really, it's okay—"

—because Mathias' urge to punish was as justified then as it is wrong now: yesterday yet another threat arrived, *Out of time Onionhead, lawyers incoming!* but he still has no answer to give and no way to respond except through Clara, *Tell him Ari's still dark, tell him I'm trying!* though Clara said *Trying doesn't mean anything to that asshole, I'll stall as long as I can.* But he must not let this be Clara's problem any longer, Clara has her own troubles to deal with; the imaginary worlds are squeezed between player bulge and revenue spiral, games announced then canceled, even some of the big ones, this week Oraculum set their dev teams adrift, is *HERO* affected too? He asked how her own *CYCLOTRONICA* was faring, but Clara said *Can't tell you, I mean I really can't. But I will say that I cashed out all my B of P shares,* which reminded him of his own shares, maybe he should cash them out before Mathias comes for him, though do what with that money?

Now a message bug lands in his field of vision, a gold-spotted beetle from Sergey, *HEY MAX, SKULL MTN,* time already for their meet? That means he has been in here all morning, he was supposed to check in with the co-op at noon. But he has a commitment to Sergey, and Sergey could know a better way to reach Ari—

—so "I need to go," he says, as Charmi shakes damp sand from her pelt, so light and soft, when he held her for those moments on the raft it was like embracing a cloud. "But I'll see you tomorrow."

"Not tomorrow," not looking at him, staring down at the sand. "I'll send a feather when I can meet."

Another silence, this one is worse, it goes on until "All right," he says, because what else can he say? in the quick steep plunge of disappointment, too steep, he should not be putting so much weight onto Charmi, emotional weight, be so attached: Charmi is here to accomplish her Yugacycle, not to be his friend, be anything to him—

—so he starts walking, not looking back, navigating over the concertina wire to the wide path between the palm trees, climbing up and up through green scrub and quicksand brambles and the slowly moving creeper vines, passing players' forms seen and unseen, who knows how many see him? on this switchback cutpath made of shining sand, it grinds underfoot like pebbled fool's gold, all the way through the foothills to the mountain of piled skulls.

And he feels what he always feels when he sees that pile, not sadness but a kind of tenderness for all those empty eyes, all the avatar deaths this game has harvested, like seeds with no place to grow. Once he had believed, with Davide, that the skulls should one day be able to sing, talk, tell their own stories in a language of their own; maybe he should tell Sergey that, Sergey who waits up there somewhere, Sergey who told him *Shooting in here is even better than fly on the wall, I'm basically pure sight. Fucking amazing, Regon was right, it's the only place to do this interview—*

—though Sergey's questions so far have been the opposite of Charmi's, not a grand overview but a zeroed-in focus, Sergey prodding and coaxing his memories, Factory memories of angry Jonas Siegler, and Mila's fierce dancer friend Katya, and Ari's enemy, the martinet Lee Davies, *You came back here for a reason,* Lee said that to him, whatever happened to Lee? Sergey asks how it felt to work there, how the staff and dancers and guests reacted and behaved, if he has been back since he left—his answer to that was no, since the building he visited with Marfa, already in its process of destruction, is not the Factory—circling again and again around the night Felix played, what was it like that night? What did he see, what really happened?

And that last is the question that makes him mum, no matter how Sergey asks it, not even when Sergey said *Full disclosure, I used to think all that spiritual stuff was made up, or delusional. I called it the woo—*

What do you call it now?

—until it hit me too. So anything you want to say about it, you can say.

But he can say nothing, not because it is hard but because it is too easy, feels too facile to say *Ari and I made a new way into reality,* that world or worlds emergent, broken and scrambled into being, situational, durational, recalling his own morning-after Factory rapture and alarm, *Do you know Krishna?* and Ari's confirmation, *Max, that was it, we made it happen*—arguing together, working together, talking together, at the breakfast dive and the noodle shop, in Deborah's little kitchen and on the Factory floor, right here in this game, *I'm the one who hired you, we're the seams*—the real reason he was at the Factory to start with, to end with, he told long-ago Teresa, there at Bitter Lake, *It's not plug and play, it's a whole world,* until finally it was, is, both.

Now "Look," Sergey calling, for once not shooting, "check this guy out," a glowing red fly the size of a real-world sparrow perched on his shoulder, its multiple wings whirring and twitching like a revved-up clockwork toy. "Another one for the nature doc."

"You don't want that, that's a goner fly. It subtracts lives—"

"What? Fuck!"

"—but you're not really playing, so it doesn't matter as much."

"I still need all the lives I can get," and Sergey shoots the fly as it flies away. "You have a good time surfing in on that sea serpent? That looked hazardous."

So Zambi is a dragonboat? Zambi is—No. No. "It was okay . . . Listen, what's going on with Ari? I keep trying to reach him but all I get is the pingback," that response so jittery and strange he cannot parse it, its visuals an oily coiling stream of bubbles, popping and reforming against a lurching, stumbling beat, and below that beat a voice, not Ari's voice, not even trying to sound human, repeating AWAY AWAY AWAY.

But Sergey only shakes his head: "I see him on Argot, but we haven't talked since Meghan's—since they left New York. You know they moved?"

AWAY AWAY, is that why Mathias is pressing him so hard? "Moved? No. Why did they move?"

"Don't know why. They did it quick, I know that. Someplace way out in the sticks."

"That music, in Ari's message—That's not Felix."

"No," unexpectedly dour, "it's not," with a sudden flap of one wing, as if something else has landed there, stealthily latched on and ready to bite. "Regon, he's going through some things right now."

INTRODUCTION TO THE YUGACYCLE
Prepared by Charmskool

Kaliyuga is the iron yuga, the time of plunder, decline, and decay. We are currently experiencing Kaliyuga.

I am documenting this yuga/time cycle, but the documentation is not a "prediction" of the "end of the world." The world does not "end." It passes through continuous cycles, until the planet becomes fully inhospitable to biochemical life.

I work in academia, but it is as a gamer that my interest in the yugacycle originates. Every yuga has primary avatars who assist the cycle's energies. As a gamer, I am foregrounding the roles of those primary avatars, because avatars are important identity markers within games, and can assist the gamer in forming/decoding/defending a personal identity in their non-gaming life as well.

These avatars develop through a series of phase transitions, much like physics, or the stages of alchemical transformation. The phases/stages are:

- Calcination and dissolution – breakdown and loss of control

- Separation – what lasts and what is discarded

- Conjunction – new merging of the conscious and unconscious

- Fermentation- suffering and resilience

- Distillation and coagulation – purification and final state of perception without dualities

Structuring a contemporary pantheon of avatars meant researching, identifying, and physically locating those avatars, a process that took longer than anticipated but yielded conclusive results:

Max Caspar, gamer and artist = KRISHNA

Krishna meditates and preserves. Krishna's time signature is KRONOS.

Ari Regon, entertainment producer = SHIVA

Shiva creates and energizes. Shiva's time signature is AION.

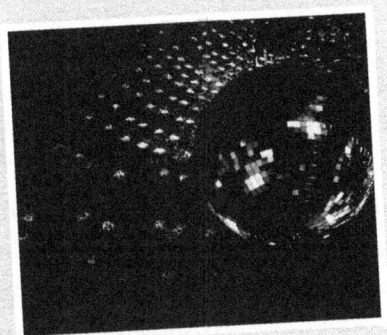

Basia Grób, corporate pharmaceuticals = KALI

Kali destroys and cleanses. Kali's time signature is KAIROS.

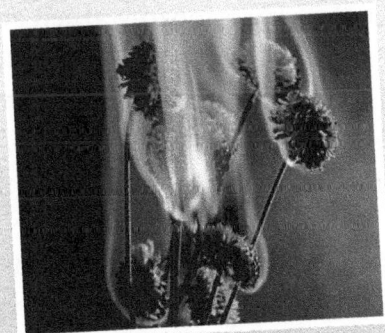

I am in ongoing consultation with Zwiebel/Max Caspar, who has made his own extensive and uniquely valuable notations available to me: on gaming history and game development, reality curation in both game and non-game environments, and the depth and range of human experience porosity. His personal experience as an avatar will be further explored and fully notated. I am very glad to have his involvement in this project.

TEN

The noon sun is a bright surprise, a day without rain in this place where it seems to rain every day. Ari slides open the black window in this fortified car, more hermetic even than an ExecuCar, like riding inside a bullet; the air recirculates every thirty seconds but he likes to keep that window open, the better to smoke, and to be seen with Basia.

Basia gets that: Basia is his weapon in play against Tom Hae, Tom Hae pinged him just as their plane took off, *Bunny Graves is on the passenger manifest? Why is she traveling with you?* so he pinged back *y not she traveled with u* as Basia sat smiling and looking out the window, even when they hit clear air turbulence and the little jet jerked and dropped like a failing elevator, and Felix yelled *Hey!* and grabbed his hand, Basia never lost her smile. He knows she enjoys thwarting Tom Hae, she waves at the guards he hired—Citadel guards, exactly what Alonzo warned against—who sit in the townhouse driveway, waiting to ferry Felix to Indigo, then waiting again in the main room while Felix works and works; he is the one who goes out, goes everywhere, alone with her.

And Basia understands how to navigate this weird and rugged, beautiful place—so much like the landscape of his dreams that it sometimes takes a minute to be sure he is awake—windbreak firs and spruce trees, roads made of asphalt and gravel and dirt, waterlogged fields and trashed gasoline cars, broken branches, broken brick, empty buildings, he has never seen so many empty buildings in his life. Just down the road from their own place sits another building technically abandoned, but fully in use as a vehicle fence yard, bullet cars and high-end trikes appearing and disappearing behind the chainlink gate, while guys in blue soccer caps wandered out to stare at the Citadel meatballs who glared back, until Basia said *I'll go talk to the neighbors.* Then the fence yard muscle turned friendly, they even broke up a break-in one rainy afternoon, lone-wolf locals looking to score some upscale DJ gear, when he went over to thank them one of the soccer caps said, *All good, bro. Your woman, Miss Boots, we speak the same language.*

Basia stays with them too, a blow-up mattress and folding table and shower pod on the ground floor of this townhouse he found and bought an hour after that throwdown fight with Felix, can it still be called a townhouse with no town around it? two stories, two and a half if you count the storage attic, very old stone and a cinderblock courtyard with dwarf fruit trees and a plug-in firepit and benches that look like they came from a bus stop, if there were any buses here, no way to get anywhere here without a car . . . Felix sometimes asks *Where do you go with her?* but he shrugs, deflects—*Around, get a feel for this place*—because if Felix knew how shaky things really are, how the platform is teetering, it would disrupt his focus, *I want to keep him clear of that, all of that,* he told Ava that once and it is more true now than ever: Felix needs to focus, and the problems are his to deal with the way they always are.

Now "You found a new coldspot?" he asks, digging out a smoke and his new lighter, chunky silver and etched with a flying crane, a Tsuru lighter he bought under the counter at the market outpost, the same place he buys these cheap and stubby black cigars, nothing like the cigars in the humidor but he likes these, they go with the territory, like this bomber jacket and fake alligator jeans, Felix said *You kind of look like a thug* and he said *Good.* "How far is it? I need to be back before Hae shows up, he's coming in from Odense. Some music museum."

"We'll be back," palming the wheel and wheeling out—Basia bought something at the curry place too, wraparound moto shades with lenses chromed a deep and gleaming blue, she said *I could drive straight into the sun with these*—"It's in a kebab joint that's a front for keno fixing," another lawless place with nearly untrace-able access, like the crusty arcade she took him to, STARCADE GAMES with an illegal boxing pit out back, and the roadside spa with empty tanning booths selling sex in ten-minute slots, and the cleaning service storefront for a black market drug depot, pre-scription drugs, she told him *Four hundred percent markup on Vismalux and they still can't keep it in stock*. Sometimes they can only use a spot once but she keeps finding more, on the low and on the fly, moving him like a counter on a board, swapping out clips to confuse the gluetrappers, never using Locate, always charging the car in the same twenty-klick radius—

—because spots like these are the only way he can guide and spur his backdoor crew, Aaron and Na Ja, Piko and Hemlock and Geraldine, the platform's PM and artists and devs already so stressed and alienated by Tom Hae and Bergeron that even money will not hold them; but the promise of fulfillment, his promise, still does, he keeps telling them *You're doing everything right, just keep going, this is all going to work*. And they believe him, the way Felix believes, Felix said *We're meant to make things that last, you're the one*—But if he fails to hold it all together, power through the shit and move the mountain, then that belief will be for nothing and this platform will die, smothered by the sheer weight of toxic C-suite ego, every meeting now is the same fucking fight—

—like yesterday's, Bergeron hitting first, hunched in his pink-and-teal eyeball, furious at the testers' latest feedback, *"Disturbing even for Matty B, redline hate vibe, why so violent"? HERO's not violent, this is a violent time! I'm not authorizing any more changes!* Then Tom Hae hit back, no more white curtains and blue sky, no sky at all in his black granite background like a prison or a cave, cold as his tone: *You're imperiling work I began decades ago, work you barely grasp. You need to reorient to reality.*

You need to grasp that reality is malleable!

Until it's litigated! Your own history proves that. Then turning that cold on him, *You approved another payout for the trailer footage. To Tutto Bene.*

Tutto Bene owns those rights. And the deadline's been pushed again. So—

Tutto Bene is your friend Sergey Kendricks. I see your friend Meghan Sorin's work destroyed itself, along with the hosting gallery, a complete waste of funds. And of course Bunny Graves is your friend now too.

And he felt himself struggle not to take that bait, felt a heat inside as he leaned back from the screen—a dominance move Jonas taught him a long time ago, sometimes he wishes he could talk to Jonas, tell Jonas *You thought shit got bad at the Factory, you should see these guys*—to say with perfect outward calm, *I'm friends with anyone who makes this platform happen.*

Now he checks again for a ping from Tom Hae, an arrival timeline, but sees only a new one from Max, **Issues with Mathias, seriously need to talk** but his hands are too fucking full right now for one of Max's philosophical deep dives, Max will have to manage his Bergeron issues by himself. And according to Sergey the shoot is going fine—

—so he looks out the window while Basia drives, cutting in and out between the commuter vehicles, the giant cannister trucks like monster versions of their own sedan, and the rickety scooters and pick-up trucks with homemade security plating, the divide between bottom and top is much starker here than in New York, or maybe he sees it better in this emptier space. The trash is different too, nothing still usable is ever thrown away, just crushed fruit liquor cartons and plastic skin-pumps for what the kids call sizzy or speedball; even the tags are different, New York tags were mostly boastful or angry but these are uniformly bleak, crossed-out skulls and crying red eyes, and everywhere the white chalk ghost of DED MANN, a local DJ, Ilias says *That spooky motherfucker's never getting into my studio, not even onto my property,* but he likes Ded Mann's mash-up of deadpan and dirge, he uses a Ded Mann track for his own away message . . . The wind whips and tangles his hair, he needs a haircut, he needs to know when Tom Hae will arrive, he needs "Coffee," to Basia, "where can we grab some?"

"There's a Kawa," tapping the map, "and a Caffé Nero right before we hit the motorway—Picture that," sharp to the car, picture what? as they pass a green trundle truck, the local equivalent of a Rite Now bot but with a human driver, and "Thomas is using rental goons," she says, "and I know I've seen that driver before. Maybe Thomas has a spy."

The photo pops up on the dash screen, he studies it, then "That's the cat food delivery guy. Good eye."

"You can't fight what you don't see . . . Just so you know, I never spied for Thomas."

"I know," because she was already busy spying for herself, Uni has confirmed what he felt in his gut from the jump, though what she really wants from him he still does not know: he knows she likes to drive him places, hook him up with what he needs, coldspots and evasive tactics, she asks for nothing, Felix says *She's different with you.* No one understands why he runs with her, trusts her, he does not understand it himself, except somehow with her he is free . . . Uni keeps sending intel meant to make him kick her to the curb, assault charges all the way back to her juvie jacket, sketchy Dive posts from masked accounts Uni says are hers, Uni told him Ines Hechman-Weir's husband was one of her sub clients and that made him laugh, he almost told Felix, he said **good 4 her hope she got big $$$.**

And early this morning Uni pinged again, as he lay awake next to still-sleeping Felix, swaddled in the plush blankets that look so out of place in this cramped and modest bedroom—

Psych Dx says unstable personality & poor impulse control
its ok not ur worry
I work 4 u. BG involvement not in ur interests imo
i keep her where i can see her anyway she gets shit done

—the wrong thing to say to Uni, he knows Uni thinks Basia is deliberately invading their own territory, spiked boots on the ground while they are just a voice in his ear, a message on his clip, if Uni knew about all the things Basia knows and has enabled, Uni would lose their shit. Meg would too, Meg is already baffled and distressed, sending a series of pointed pings, *What is your thought process here? She is CHAOS. Stay in charge!* Even Sergey weighed in, *Things going good with Max C. Bunny G still hanging on?*

And the day they left New York, Alonzo took him aside, to shake hands and say *It was a pleasure working with you and Mr. Perez.*

Not my call to let you go, you know that.

Your company's paying for EP, it's their decision. But whoever they hire, you want to watch out for the meatballs, meatballs will get you into more trouble than they'll get you out of. Zero mitigation skills, with professional distaste, and a kind of kindly worry: of all the mistakes Tom Hae has made this one ranks near the top, sacrificing watchful, careful Alonzo to Bergeron's pouting fanboy spite, Bergeron still pissed that Alonzo had blocked him from Felix on that useless weekend trip.

Then Alonzo said *Mr. Regon, about Miss Graves*—And though Alonzo did not know Basia's real name, and could not define what Basia was doing during those lunches and shopping trips and backgammon games, still Alonzo did not trust her, Alonzo said *She asked Mr. Perez questions about you, and a few times she followed him, I saw her on the street. I've been trained in risk assessment, and in my opinion Miss Graves is a risk.*

Did you tell Felix that? Or Tom Hae?

I'm telling you, Mr. Regon.

"Alonzo talked to me about you, before he left. He said you asked Felix a lot of questions."

"I asked him about you, you know that. And I asked about his music."

Felix does not understand why she is here, Felix was surprised when she tossed her bag in the ExecuCar behind the movers' truck, *Bunny's coming with us?* though Felix did not ask why, too relieved to be leaving, escaping whatever hovering threat, whatever drove the fight about the gallery opening—a serious fight, Felix shouting *Do you have a fucking death wish? Don't you care about me at all?* and his own shout back *Why can't you just say what you mean?*—that fight somehow part of the constant questions, as if he was a teenager coming home late, where had he been, who was he talking to, who gave him this or that? questions he stopped trying to answer and started to ignore, which made things worse, but no answer could ever be good enough to make those questions stop.

Yet as soon as they landed here, Felix relaxed; the very first night Felix took him up to the roof, flat brown shingles and old peeling rubber insets, moss puddles and a cracked plastic stool, and *We're home*, Felix said, *finally. And look, you can see all the stars!* then kissed him, fucked him right there on that roof, dirty and perfect, it felt like they had been there before, would always be there, spellbound in pleasure, the dark world sparked with stolen headlights below and stars high above, so many more stars here to see; afterward they held each other as a colder wind came on, shivering, smiling, neither of them wanted to get dressed and go back down . . . Felix seems happy in a way he has not been since before Quest Fest, maybe even longer: happy in bed, happy to brew morning tea and bitch about the whiskey choices at the market, cheap Red Rose and even cheaper Cesarz, happy to swim in the janky little lake that lies just past the woods on the Indigo property, brown water and green mud, sometimes Karim swims with him though Gus says *No thanks, there's no vax for that water yet.* And most of all Felix is happy with the depth of the quiet, in the water, on the roof, under the stars, *I can hear everything here,* Felix says. *Everything.*

Felix even found a cat, or the cat found him, in the scrub field across from their place, covered in burrs but walking like a model, a small striped cat with darker stripes around her eyes. Felix calls that her eyeliner, Felix calls her Andromeda, and fusses over her, she has a tracking collar and her own padded window perch and special food delivered, Felix said *She can't eat that junk from the market, that junk is full of bones.*

She probably ate rats in that field.

She lives with us now. I'm taking care of her.

Most of all Felix is happy with the hours and days he spends at Indigo, old-school decks and 12 Tonez interface and haptic speakers and even newer, better Round Sound headphones, the studio redecorated in his honor with balsam candles and blue bead hangings made from *Lapis lazuli,* Ilias said, *it's the stone of inner visions, it activates the third eye chakra. Oh and it's against the evil eye!* Gus and Karim laugh about that, call it Indigo Bead Studio, but they call Felix "St. Perez," joking yet not joking, Karim told him *After Dark Park, people camped out in that field, they used to dance to try to make Felix come back;* all of them seem to see something new in Felix, something they need to live up to, to be able to work with him again.

And on his own trips to the studio, not often but he goes when he can, he sees that rapt, sweet frown, hears Felix using everything he has, his beats, the piano's shimmer and prowl, that endless spool of sounds—last time he heard their old apartment's HVAC mutter, and the syncopated clatter of chains from the fence yard, Andromeda's rough purr, even a breakfast orange, those almost noiseless moist explosions of peel separating from fruit—this is what Felix has been trying so hard for so long to do, not only hear, not only channel the pure voice of the hum, but access its flow, *I play music, it's in us* . . . Felix is inside the hum, now.

"Felix loves working here."

"That's why you came, isn't it? For his music."

"It's not just music."

"I know," not agreement but shared conviction, he knows she means it, she plays Felix's sets every time they drive, obscure sets sometimes, things even he does not remember, what does that music mean to Basia? Does she like to dance? and "Music existed before anything else," she says, "even time. Felix told me that once . . . There's Caffé Nero."

Inside the café is steamy, sun beating through rooftop windows, and in the line other customers glance at them, stare at them, a few point their clips, do those people think they see a couple? what kind of couple? Her boots and his smile . . . They order their drinks to go, a double espresso and a bottle of Pflaume Thé, gold foil label with a golden plum, he has never heard of that brand before so back in the car "Can I try?" he asks, then takes a drink, a mouthful so sour he can barely spit it out the window. "Whoa, that shit's worse than Limonale!"

She laughs, takes the bottle back. "It's an acquired taste."

The espresso reeks of chicory filler, he sips, then dumps that out the window too. "How did you acquire it?"

"On family trips," taking her own sip, pulling back on the motorway ramp. "The Sistine Chapel, the part they don't let tourists see, I went there. And Jajce, the Mithraeum, the rubble of it anyway, builders found it when they were digging a new house foundation, I went there too, and the next day I saw the bas relief of Mithras killing the sacred bull, it's in the Museum Wiesbaden, it's fucking depressing. And I went to Sylvia Plath's grave—'Eternity bores me, I never wanted it,' Sylvia Plath said that."

He thinks of Genie, *I grew up in hotels,* he has no clue who Sylvia Plath might be. "Your family took a lot of trips."

"The best trip was the one that got me away from them. From my mother's apartment," swerving, deliberately cutting off a cannister truck that blares its alarm in their wake. "Can I try one of your cigars?"

"Wait till we stop, it'll probably make you dizzy. You don't like your mom?"

"She was—weak. What about yours?"

"Ava, yeah, she's great."

The kebab shop is smaller than he expected, just a hole in the wall with soccer posters papering its windows, on a street with a hospital clinic at one end and a busy bar at the other, a church in-between with an angel statue stationed at its doors, the marble gray and grainy as freezer ice. Two INX scooters are parked outside the shop—precinct police, local authority untethered to law; cappies, what do they call them here, flips, the flips are one of the few real dangers of this place, and the drone flyers who chase people, not to rob, just to terrorize, Basia told him they were army surplus and he said *The drones? Or the guys flying them?* and she said *Both*—and inside two youngish men in brown uniforms sit at the short yellow counter, chewing kebabs and laughing with the counter guy, shaved head and a Diego Diablo jersey, the laughter stops when they walk in.

"Is Marius here?" Basia asks.

No one answers. The men look at her and at him, then at each other. Basia unzips her shoulderpack halfway, to show a fat fold of paper, money, cash.

"Marius," she says. "Is he here."

The counter guy smirks, the flips resume eating—and everyone jumps, he jumps too as Basia slaps her hand flat on the counter, one of the flips knocks his lager glass right into his plate and "We're not here for lunch," she says, "or keno. What's the password, Marius?" dropping bills beside the pooling mess until Marius plucks them up, Marius says, "This spot's ice cold. Double that."

"The rest when we're finished. What's the password?"

Logging in, he keeps his back to the wall while she stands beside him, hands loose, this place feels the way it feels when trouble is starting at the club. He forces himself to ignore that, ignore the men's stares and concentrate as he checks in with Aaron and Na Ja, approving their new and riskier workarounds, warning them to expect a major blow-up between Tom Hae and Bergeron, *shits going 2 fly brace 4 impact*, telling them he has a *live TH meet ✓ back 2nite* then logging out, scrubbing out, and "OK," his murmur to her. "Done."

"Just keep walking," her murmur back, unzipping her shoulderpack, pausing at the counter—

—but as he tries to pass, one of the flips grabs his elbow, thumb digging in at the tendon, a numb little pain and "Rich man," the flip says, acne scars and a sneer. "Fancy girl, fancy car."

"You want the money?" Basia says to Marius, voice flat. "Or what."

"Rich man, let's see what you got in your pockets—"

—and suddenly a kebab plate is airborne, smashing in a blast of crockery and greasy meat, Basia hurls another like a discus as Marius ducks below the counter, and as he jerks his arm free Basia knocks the flip sideways, shouting to him "Go, *go!*" while Marius reappears, something dark in hand, is that a gun? The door seems a hundred miles away, he sprints, one of the men screams, Basia snarls *"Siktir git!"* and he hears a sound, what is that sound, the car is already running when he jumps inside, the empty tea bottle rolls out into the street—

—then Basia is there, slamming the car into drive, flinging a handful of bills out the window, her blue shades are gone, her chin is bleeding and "Hang on," she says, "we're going *this* way," down a dogleg side road that seems to dead end in a little field, it does dead end but they keep going, the car jouncing and bucking through weeds and over rocks, they hit a ditch and his head hits the ceiling, the car's undercarriage scrapes and grinds—

—then the tires finally find asphalt, a feeder road where they swerve and merge and finally slow and "Ow," he says, "my fucking head," then laughs, and she laughs too, the laughter of escape and release, wiping at her face with the t-shirt's hem, that shirt already splashed with blood and something else, something brown, the shirt says ARRIVED HAPPY LEFT NOT and "Are you okay?" he says. "What the fuck happened back there?"

"I'm fine," making a face, comic, unexpected, a troublemaker's shrug, he laughs again, then "'Siktir git,'" he says, "that's Turkish. You speak Turkish?"

"A little. Serap taught me—"

"Serap," his smile fading, Serap is his mother's name—

"—and I know you speak it too. I know a lot about you, Ari, not everything but a lot. And you know me—"

"Why?" still pierced by memory—Serap's perfect Turkish coffee in the china cups, Serap who was more beautiful than anyone, saying *I want you to have everything, everything that's yours,* Serap who left and never came back—"Why are you here? What do you want?"

"I want to make things happen. With you—"

"What things—"

"Everything—"

—and he stares at her, he takes out one cigar then another, lights it up for her, the car fills with smoke and "Volume," she shouts, "volume, *volume!*" as his clip pings, Felix, Felix agitated because **wtf Hae was here!? going 2 our place???** so "Get us back," he says, and she does, blowing past the other traffic, the road flying by, not like a dreamscape but like another memory, the teenage smiler who shanked him, his blood and the snow and shaking, shaking in the speeding rush of life, *better than alive*—

—and at the townhouse two Citadel cars are already parked and waiting, flanking a mud-splashed silver sedan, before Basia fully brakes he is out. Tom Hae stands beside that car, wearing another square-shouldered suit, uneven black stripes on chalky white: and in this real-life sunlight, without the shielding mercy of a screen, Tom Hae's strangeness is even more glaring, all those rooms and all of them empty, nothing there but a stare. And Tom Hae says, as if they are already in conversation, "I'll assume you know the difference between aleatory uncertainty and epistemic uncertainty?"

"You're way early."

"The museum was closed, I visited the Domkirke instead—Of course you're here," as Basia approaches, her face already swelling, the fresh lipstick makes her mouth look bloody too. "Tour guide to the gutter—"

"Hello, Thomas. You look like a barcode."

"—boxing rings, seedy spas, I suppose the next stop is a leather bar—"

—and Basia's glance flicks to him, and his to her, Tom Hae knows where they go but not what they do there—

"—while Mr. Perez is in the studio, trying to work. But Mr. Perez just refused to see me, because he feels so uncertain of the process."

"Uncertainty," his own voice as calm as it has ever been, though in his chest is a rising pressure, adrenaline churn, and heat, the heat fueled by Basia standing beside him, her hands behind her back, all the Citadel meatballs are staring at her now. "That's right, Felix needs stability. The devs need it, the artists need it, the whole platform needs—"

"I continued to believe I had leveraged a workable team, even when you insisted on moving to your little clubhouse," with a scornful sideways nod at the townhouse. "But now—Bergeron's last supper, you've seen it?"

"His what?" as the linki hits his clip, Basia looking over his shoulder at a hyper-cartoonlike image, a wall painting, is that a real wall? a mural of smiling Bergeron in a dark purple suit with a curling purple tentacle tie, sitting at a long table next to Felix who wears a giant golden headphone halo; the rest of the painted-in people he does not recognize, except for Derek Ferris, Derek crouched at the table's end with a dripping cartoon paintbrush, Derek made the mural at Silver Landings and this is his work too—

"Bergeron put himself in the Iscariot position, that fool has no idea! He's a grease stain on God's tablecloth! So it's time to put an end to uncertainty. Effective midnight UTC, Bergeron is no longer part of the platform."

"You—Wait," in plunging disbelief, this is not strategy, not any kind of management move, this is insanity, this will obliterate the devs, smother the PM and artists with impossible demands, his crew all waiting to hear from him, trusting him. And Felix—"You're forcing Bergeron out? How's that going to work? How will we keep the gamers involved, how—"

"And your own grasp of real-making, how real-making is essential for an interface that serves the individual seeker—"

"God hates a martyr, Thomas."

"—I believed that represented a critical value exchange, despite any issues I might have with you personally, your calculating, provocative behavior. But by isolating Mr. Perez, you attack the platform. My platform. So effective immediately, you are no longer chief belief officer at Insomnious."

He stares at Tom Hae, who clearly expects some explanation, plea, response, something, but when he finally speaks from inside that heat it comes out very cold: "You still pray that serenity prayer? The one about climbing out of your own asshole?"

And Tom Hae's stare back is deeply ugly, Tom Hae turning back to the silver car, the Citadel guards following. As that car pulls away, Ari's clip pings, executive channel from Insomnious HR with a separation notice, Insomnious legal with a link to his NDA, *you can always walk away whenever you want* but not this time, this platform is his gift to Felix, and power is power—

—and when he turns to Basia he sees her smiling, someone else might be afraid of her now, afraid of that smile, but when she says "Where to," it is not a question—

—and while she speeds to Indigo, gravel flying, he pings Felix, pings again, Felix does not answer, why? pinging one last time as they pull up, bumping over the crusted runnels of mud, sunlight still on the crabapple trees and machine ruins and driveway Jeep, on Ilias outside squinting over a blunt, letting it drop as "Your money guy was here," Ilias' worried shrug, "but Felix said don't let him in, so I didn't. Is everything cool?"

Inside it smells like burned wax, the balsam candles guttering, the studio light unlit, and Felix sits at the long refectory table, his clip on that table beside a cluster of mostly empty wine bottles and a metal bowl of black plums. The two Citadel guards slouch at the table's other end, one looks half-asleep, the other stares through a Quirk until "Hey," Basia says to them, "schedule change. You can go."

"What?" says the one without the Quirk, sitting up straighter. "Who's taking the shift?" then taking a closer look at her, "We're going to need some confirmation—"

"Confirm it out there," standing over them, staring down until Felix nods, and they rise, they leave, the door closes and "Bunny," Felix says, "Basia, why didn't you ever tell me your real name is Basia? I thought I knew who you were—And where the fuck were *you*?"

She looks, not at Felix, but at him. "I'll be outside."

And as the door opens and closes again, "You never told me," Felix says, "where you go with her. Looks like someplace exciting—a boxing pit? Hae knew about that, he pinged me about it, so I added it to the list. It's a long list—"

—skidding the clip across the table, it hits the fruit bowl with a metallic chime like a furious little bell, he sees his own string of pings still blinking there unread. And in his chest the heat spikes, a burning impatience with Felix's endless tantrums, especially now when everything is in freefall and they need, yes, stability, Felix needs to stay in the studio while he somehow makes a way to make this work, forces a way if he has to, this will happen so "I don't know what you mean," he says. "And I don't have time—"

"When do you ever have time! I barely see you—"

"—because I'm working, I'm doing my best! For you, we came here for you—"

"For us! This is our home. Or do you miss New York? Do you miss—"

"—so you need to stay here, and work—"

"And where are you going to be?" and when he does not answer, because he has no answer yet, Felix shoves back from the table, rises, turns away, turns back again as if directionless, lost, and "Does Bunny know?" Felix cries. "Does every fucking body know but me? And I got hit on all the time, *all the time,* but I never—"

"What?"

"—Julian Zero, his little *tune,* 'I watch you sleep,' you danced with him, you dance with everybody! All those DJ boys, that little shit Antwan, did you dance with Ded Mann too? You don't know what it's like to feel this way, you don't know—"

"No I don't," finally angry, can this seriously be Felix's trouble, all this time? all those arguments and questions, just stupid suspicion—Julian Zero? Antwan *Layne?*—and all of it a total insult to their love, *together no matter where we are, we need to trust each other,* what happened to that love and trust? He loves Felix, he will always love Felix. "You're just inventing bullshit over nothing."

As Felix turns away again, he sees that someone, Ilias? has taped up beside the studio door that little prayer card, the Christopher card; and he remembers his talk with Ava, when Felix was pursued by Jason Rice, greedy Jase who tried and failed to take Felix and his music, Ava said *You'll take care of him, he's yours.* So "I don't miss New York," trying hard to keep his voice even, trying even for a smile. "What I miss is having lunch with Ava."

"I don't," Felix turning back, not returning the smile, rubbing at his chin. "But then I'm not in a romcom with her like you are."

"Jesus! At least I'm nice to her—"

"You would be, she's the mother you never had—"

"What—Felix, what the *fuck*—"

"I—Ari, I didn't mean that, I'm sorry—Ari I'm *sorry*—"

—as he slams out of the room and outside, Basia in some dispute with the meatball guards but everybody stops when they see him, when he says "Drive—"

—and Felix in the doorway now, Felix shouting something but he has already closed the car door, closed the black window, only Basia hears and Basia says nothing, only drives, passing the townhouse turnoff for the motorway, silence heavy in the car until finally she asks, "Where to?"

"I don't know." His hands are trembling, he lights up, draws hard through the heat and the hurt, astonishing hurt, he never talks about his mother, ever, Felix is the only one who knows, the only one he trusted—"I want coffee. Espresso. Italian espresso, no fucking chicory."

"There's a club, Peitsche, they're 24/7 and they'll get anything you want. It'll take a minute to get there, though."

"I don't have anyplace else to be."

"'Fate is cruel and men are wretched.'"

"Who said that, Sylvia Plath?"

"Schopenhauer. And my grandmother. Let's go—"

—the car accelerating, his clip pinging, pinging, pinging, smoke in his mouth, his heart on fire.

FATE IS CRUEL AND MEN ARE WRETCHED.
—ARTHUR SCHOPENHAUER

ELEVEN

They stand side by side on the caged-in mezzanine, watching the lone staffer pass between the dancefloor tables, gathering empty wine bottles and sugarpop poppers and ripped wrist thongs, sweeping up clumps of wet straw, Peitsche in the morning is a quiet place. Ari looks beyond tired, still wearing the t-shirt the club's owner gave him—tight and black, with the Peitsche tagline, *Estoy vivo bebé*—that owner, Esther, so thrilled to have Ari Regon in her sex club that she comped them both for everything, *Vielen Dank, Bunny! I was a Dark Factory power user, a Y user, it's special to meet him in the flesh.*

And as he rubs his eyes, "It's always the same guy," Ari says, "I'm chasing him but I never catch him, I always wake up first . . . Dreams are weird."

"I never remember mine—*Ah*," wincing at the pain in her jaw as she yawns—

—because neither of them slept for long, already dawn when they came back to this suite from that half-moon table at the edge of the dancefloor, where they sat through the rotating DJ sets, each with its own deferential shoutout to Ari, shoutouts he acknowledged with the barest lift of his glass, then through the busy determined fucking that followed, it took over most of that dancefloor, the first night's theme was slip'n'slide, last night's was broomstick. And both nights Ari drank oil-black Italian espresso, then Baraky whiskey, and smoked and watched the people who tried to engage his attention, asked him to chat or to dance; he danced with no one, spoke very little, smiled even less. At Peitsche clips are deactivated—the door staff dunks them in lube if people complain—and no Auras or Quirks are allowed, Ari approved of that, he said *It's like not being here at all,* and he is definitely elsewhere, angry in a way she did not anticipate, as if his anger is a mountain, an unscalable alp, and he stands alone atop it, staring down.

The only time he seemed truly engaged was when the server brought his whiskey and her Cabernet along with an extra glass—without asking, they know her here—and he asked, eyebrows up, *Who's that for?*

I always—It's for ZZ.

Who's ZZ?

My friend . . . Girlfriend.

She's joining us?

She's dead.

And he nodded, he waited till she poured her wine then touched his glass to hers, then to the empty glass, a gesture of such kindness that she felt her throat go tight, the sudden glottal clench before a sob; and she thought of Felix, seeing again in her mind's eye Felix in the Indigo doorway, his face, his stricken shout, *You're taking him, where are you taking him?* because at that moment Felix finally understood, not what she had done but that she had done it, she was the one, her own stare back did not deny.

And as they drove away, her clip began to ping with Argot and Kerosene blocks, from GusBurnsBeats and SolidK, IndigoIsMusic, and finally Felix himself; she kept waiting for Felix to ping Ari, or call him, tell him, but if Felix tried, Ari did not respond, Ari is answering no pings from anyone . . . Last night Esther asked her *You're still a backgammon shark?* and she nodded, in backgammon they would call what she accomplished *coup classique,* a match that appeared unwinnable now firmly and definitively won: Ari is isolated from everything and everyone but her. And now they can do what she knows he can do, his combustible energy loosed against everything that deserves its force, Thomas, Agni, the whole sickened world, and her velocity will drive it as far as it can go—

—and from the hallway "May we serve?" two of the daylight

staff, severely pretty in kitchen whites which at Peitsche are black, carrying in the brunch buffet: steel plates of passionfruit and currants, croissants and crêpes, curling twists of seasoned turnip that smell like steak frites, espresso and spring water and a liter of dry champagne. Her own appetite surprises her, everything tastes good, though Ari eats nothing, only drinks the coffee, sips the champagne, until one of the servers asks, "Would you prefer something else for brunch, sir?"

"Brunch for me is usually a smoke. What I really need," turning to her, plucking at the alligator jeans, "is to change these clothes."

"Me too. This thing feels like a surgical appliance," the black rubber vest Esther gave her to wear, she threw away the ruined ARRIVED HAPPY t-shirt and bloodstained sports bra as soon as they got here—

—from the kebab shop foray that already feels unreal as a bad dream, she knew the minute they walked in that spot was a mistake, her mistake. And when Marius went for the gun, she was stunned by her own jolting fear—a new emotion, no fight before has ever scared her, not because of the weapon but because she has someone to protect, the way she tried to protect ZZ, her failure a tragedy that will never end—she screamed at Ari to run, then speared the fallen flip through something fleshy, forearm, leg, and the flip still standing punched her in the face, her driving glasses flew off and the world lost its protective blue, turned to grubby color, mostly red, mostly blood, some of it hers, she heard herself shout *Fuck off!* as she kicked that second flip in the dick and Marius fired, the bullet hit the wall and she hit the car's start switch, she meant to throw the money as she ran, as a distraction, but forgot till she got to the street, so intent on getting Ari safely away—

—and "They can get you fresh clothes," her nod to the servers, "someone will go out to the shops. Correct?"

"Oh ja, yes! We're food service, but we can notify hospitality right away."

"Give me your sizes, Ari."

And within the hour "These are really nice," Ari modeling the black vented trackpants—seaweed silk, the black pullover is stretch linen—before they head out, without discussion, to the car, the road, the townhouse.

At first the drive back is silent, down the bland avenues that cloak Peitsche, fenced streetside greenery and two-story office buildings, the gated cluster of shops, but when they hit the motorway "Play something," Ari says, and she does: not Felix's beats—she cannot listen to Felix now—but Bach's cello suites, recorded at the bottom of a mineshaft in the Urals, the cello sounds as if it is fighting its way back to the light.

As she drives, Ari checks his clip and answers, answers, answers, no more coldspots needed, he does not look up until they near the turnoff for Indigo, passing the grungy little market, the clinic and pharmacy and "You have any ink?" he asks. "We—I got this there," turning his wrist to show her the stars, that line of three like Orion's belt. "For a while I was going to get another one, to cover up my scar."

Surprised, "What scar?" and when he shakes his head, not *no* but *not now*, "I have scars. I made this one myself," displaying her forearm, in this car's light the heart looks particularly livid, like dead flesh grafted on. "Thomas lectured me on Aztec autoscarification, but it really sicked him out. Thomas doesn't understand pain, he only likes to inflict it."

"I'm seeing that, yeah. He just rebranded the platform, a shitty 24-hour rebrand, now it's called 'Sunyata'—"

"'The void.'"

"—and according to Insomnious I quit *and* I'm fired, they're threatening to sue the shit out of me, breach of contract, IP endangerment, Aliyah said it just goes on and on. And Uni said Bergeron's suing Insomnious, Uni said his mansion just fell into the ocean, they said he almost fell in with it . . . Everything's falling apart," accurate, unfazed, turning back to his clip as the cello turns to a stoic solo piano, some unknown tune like a ragtime death march, until they pull up to the townhouse, its empty driveway, and "No one's here," she says.

Inside everything is silent, the ground floor curtains are closed, cups sticky in the sink, the cat's dishes are gone; Felix is gone. In her own room, she sees the blow-up bed's sheets stripped to a pile on the floor, though nothing else has been touched or moved, the backgammon board still sits on the folding table, its checkers placed for a game. The shower is cold, but it feels good to exchange the clammy rubber vest for her Schiphol hoodie and workout pants, before tending to her aching jaw, another pain patch and a makeshift icepack, dish gel and water half-frozen in a zipper bag.

Stretching against the courtyard benches, she scans her own clip, watching Bergeron's concrete altar of a house collapse into the Adriatic—dramatic, almost operatic, destruction can be beautiful—one of a line of mansions battered and sunk by a huge *bura* storm, how did Unicorn16 know Bergeron was inside when it happened? On Insomnious' site is a different kind of destruction, the mountain is gone, the sun is gone, nothing is there but a golden rim made of a burning word, SUNYATA; no statement has been posted about Ari, all the assaults are coming from their anonymous poison streams, half a dozen up and gushing, the newest post says Felix is filing for divorce, that cruelty is definitely a Thomas touch. Ari's defenders are posting back, mostly on Argot, but his haters on Dive are in overdrive, especially someone whose handle is UXKing41, obsessively tagging everything *#regonfail*—

—and now "Take a look," Ari beside her in the courtyard, humidor cigar in one hand, clip in the other. "Na Ja just sent this—"

—a gated linki for a private party, *Exclusive performance by a nonpareil musical genius, enter SUNYATA, creative black tie,* and "Terribly Keen," she says, recognizing the ridiculous pursed-lips logo. "Terribly Keen is Gerald Baumpierre, he's done events for Thomas before. You want to go to this?"

"Hae won't talk to me—this way could work. If we can get in."

"We can crash. But let me try something," scrolling through the list of Thomas' passwords, locked out from the master list, all the big things, but she can still access his New York barber service and

Sportshalle membership, his Cobblers' Row tailor account—and the Terribly Keen client-only portal, the invitation, and "We're in," showing him the bright blinking gold dot, *CONFIRMED REGINA SALVE*. "You're my plus-one."

"'Regina Salve'?"

"It was my domme name. My title was relationship auditor."

"You must have scared the shit out of Mr. Ines," with a sudden smile, his first in days. "Nice work . . . What is this place, Nouvelle Terre?"

"I don't know, but I'll find out," then "'Musical genius,'" carefully. "That must mean Felix is playing."

"That's what it says," no smile now but no more anger either, is his gaze pain? or something else, something deeper that is neither? He blows a perfect smoke ring, another, watches them float and disappear, and "Genie taught me that," he says. "Genie loved Felix a lot . . . I'll tell Na Ja we're going."

Back to her workout, she considers the event venue—bizarre even by Thomas' standards, Nouvelle Terre is an isolated bunker, rated for life-sustainment during and after civil unrest, climate disaster, NBC events, nuclear biological chemical, with its own water system and armed security—then runs through all the visible approaches and exits, maps and drone shots, while she runs the wet and empty road, hearing only her own breathing, the percussive grind of the gravel, the sudden weedy rustle when her passage spooks some animal too swift for her to see; for the first time in her life, as she runs, nothing is chasing her.

And as dusk comes on, she stops by the fence yard, to enlist the soccer cap guys as partners in her combat tune-up, leapfrog and stun spins and burn fence top-outs, the yard owner watches until "Miss Boots," he says, "you really got those lazy bastards hopping. You ever need a short-term vehicle, I'll hook you up."

"I could use something rugged for the weekend."

"Off-road? Done."

In the morning a hybrid trike is parked outside the townhouse, no-puncture tires and a gaudy gold finish, it gleams even in the fitful sun as she takes it for a shakedown drive through bumpy fields, pavement changes and muddy sudden swerves, the trike rocks but never tips. On the way back, she stops at the market outpost for a new pair of driving shades, lime green this time, and a double order of hot rice and curried lentils, stowing the bag in the clamshell compartment as a Jeep slows to park beside her—

—the black Jeep from Indigo, and at the wheel Felix in a pink ballcap, a Citadel guard beside him. When Felix sees her, he swings the Jeep wide, to park as far away as possible across the little lot, and she feels the same hard dismay as on their moving day, she wants to say something to Felix, say what? *I'm sorry?* She is not sorry, she did exactly what she planned to do.

On the drive back she turns to his music, like a one-sided conversation, an invocation, the sets choosing themselves, ones she knows, ones she has never heard before, playing all day long till she climbs, finally, into the blow-up bed, still listening—a pair of his early gigs, at places called Temple Club and Thanx 4 Nothing, those beats so raw and reaching, reaching, incomplete, his life before Ari—and that dismay now almost overwhelming, what is this, is this guilt? She cannot be guilty, she needed Ari, *the right arena for your skills*—

—and waking just after dawn, still listening, his airport concert playing now, the clunky public piano, Erik Satie's *Gnossienne No. 1*, and her face is wet, she is crying, why? because the whole world is in Felix's music, a world of beauty swamped by a storm of pain, and Felix should not play this music in Thomas' sick hermetic tumulus, Felix should not play for Thomas at all. But Thomas has him now, has him alone, she made that happen—

—and upstairs, Ari is awake, shirtless and making coffee, before he turns she sees the scar on his back, a knife scar for sure, twisty and pink. And "Hey," he says, surprised by her, then by her tears, "what's up, what's wrong?"

On the little wooden table, by the glossy green ashtray, is a card, the prayer card, the black Madonna with the red-slashed face. And "Sara-la-Kali," she says, "the Lady of Częstochowa—they shot arrows at her, they sliced her with a sword. Her statue should have been up at the shrine—"

"What shrine?"

—and without knowing she will, without being able to stop, she tells him about the shrine and the truck-fuckers, Serap sharing vodka in a beat-up travel mug, Serap saying *Teach me how you do them without touching!* because that was the way to exercise power, that was why she was there until "He hit me," she says, "he slammed my head against the window, so I stabbed him. I stabbed him and he bled like a fucking fountain, I thought I killed him—"

—and in Ari's eyes she sees no censure or surprise, only respect: "You took down both those flips, I never saw anybody move so fast. And the other guy, that counter guy, he had a gun?"

"He did. But he missed."

"He shot at us?" and when she nods, "You saved my ass," brushing her bruised jaw with his thumb, the hand with the ring, his wedding ring—

—and again the warm shock, the way it felt when they first shook hands, but so much warmer now, core to core and "I've been fighting all my life," she says. "I won't let anyone hurt you."

"Miracle worker . . . You keep that card."

And the card is in her jacket pocket, next to her lipstick, the jenny knife in the thigh pocket of the black tac pants, when they leave for the event in the cooling and unsettled afternoon, clouds building in the west, it will rain before dark. Ari is amused by the trike—"Slick ride, you really want us to make an entrance—" then thoughtful when the music starts, another deliberate choice, her choice of the Jericho set, an alternate mix by a DJ called NYC NIA; he listens until "AltFest9000," he says. "There never was another AltFest, Lars Lindberg got forced out, the producer. Everybody else was too scared."

"You weren't."

"I wasn't there. I was working for Your Own Eyes, until they let me go. Jonas let me go too . . . Meg still owns A Walk in the Park."

The wind picks up as they leave the long feeder road for the hills, and she turns off the music, the better to hear what waits for them past the last-chance charging station and takeaway liquor shop, in the foothills carpeted with witchgrass, dotted with scrub pines and dwarf beech, a few ancient doorless lean-tos like roosts for ghosts, but they see no other vehicles, they see no one at all. She brought a polycutter for smart fences, but all she needs is a bolt cutter to enter the fenced and posted private land, sign after sign warning *NO TRESPASSING/ENTRÉE INTERDITE* and "The event space," she says, "will have bad décor. And a lot of guns—"

"*Arrêt!* Stop!" loud from an unseen sensor placed somewhere in a tree, as a gate slides up from the roadbed. "This is a non-approved entrance. *Arrêt!* Stop! This is a non-approved—"

"Hang on," brisk, pointing the trike not toward the gate but down through the crackle of brush, rolling over rocks and crawling past boulders, following the fencing from the outside, until "Here," she says, "here's our entrance," climbing up again to a maintenance and delivery gate where a rose pink truck, BRILLIANT BUBBLES, is entering, she guns the trike inside before that gate can close.

And immediately "Where are we?" she calls to the approaching gate guards, one tall and one short, drab unmarked uniforms, visibly armed. "Where's the performance?"

The guards stare—the gaudy trike, Ari's hair scrambled wild by the wind, her gleaming lime green shades, definitely not black tie—and "You're guests?" the short guard asks, as the taller one checks her clip invite; it pings. "Ms., uh, Salvay?"

"We're guests," staring back, this guard will be the problem if there is a problem; beside her, Ari stays quiet. "And we're missing the performance."

"You don't have the event wristbands. And the other guests arrived at the hotel helipad—"

"Clearly this isn't a helicopter. And we're *missing the performance*," with an authority so absolute that the tall guard powers up a security trike, less rugged than their own, to lead them off through the leafy compound, the shorter guard watching them go—

—and "I thought," Ari says, "you were going to run that guy over."

"I did. Look, there it is," the sloping bunker, built into a hill and designed to be invisible, but the wheaty, framing weeds are too uniform, the camouflage grass too green, and before what must be the entrance sits a golden party tent, its rippling sides like a breathing beast's, with tall doorside stands of yellow ranunculus and black fern. When the guard drives off, she carefully repositions their trike two meters from that tent's door, as Ari hops out, brushing back his hair with both hands, sunglasses tucked to his collar, his gaze to hers: "Ready?"

"How's this going to go?"

"I don't know. But I don't think we'll be here long—Hey, hi," his smile for the handsome doorway greeter, gold tux and blond fade, the greeter's smile lingers as Ari murmurs in her ear, "Thought you said they'd have bad décor—"

—and inside she does not see Thomas, or Felix, or any set-up for Felix, that must be in the bunker itself, its half-draped entrance just beside the lavish wet bar. A gold-suited bartender mixes cocktails while a shaven-headed helper, serviette jammed in one pocket, totes in a rose pink case of champagne, and circling servers offers individual plates of Terribly Keen's terrible hors d'oeuvres, something yellow with yellow sauce. Gerald Baumpierre is there, in black tie with a black beret—he does not recognize her—along with the usual wealthy slumming crowd, but there is a new edge here, a whiff of dark euphoria, hysteria, do any of these people really believe they can hide from the end of the world? Do they know it already happened—

"—because an asteroid is coming from deep space, it's called Apropos. And everything it hits, it kills—"

"Invest a million, waste a million. The only safe strategy is aquacapture—"

"—met at that bondage ashram in Bogotá—"

"—or gold, you'll never go wrong with gold—"

"—Flower People, it was intense! We followed him *everywhere*—"

—and Ari's muttered sigh, "This asshole," because that barback helper, she sees now, is Jason Rice, how is Jason Rice here? Thomas never gives second chances. And just beside the bar, off the rack in sparkly boots like a dildo in the punchbowl, is Antwan Layne: she sees Antwan Layne see her, a flash of fear and deep dislike, but still he hurries over, crowing "Ari! You look amazing! I sent you my Zipper linki, did you see it?"

Now Jason Rice is heading their way too, with a fixed and hateful look, so she puts herself in his path, she says, "Did Thomas whistle you back?" and "Tom Hae?" Jason Rice says, to her, to himself, to no one: this close she can tell that Jason Rice is seriously high on something, his shoulders are up around his ears and he smells like night sweats beneath the duty-free cologne. "Hae fired me, so fuck him. And fuck that prick Ari Regon, *he's* fired now, he's a failure!" *#regonfail,* so Jason Rice must be UXKing41. "And I have a new précis. For Minos—"

—as music starts from somewhere inside the bunker, not Felix's music, not live, some symphony recording of, what is that? then "Fuck," her own mutter, because this is Wagner's *Götterdämmerung,* the hero's death march, this is a very bad sign. Or a nod from the universe, her own nod, because no matter what else happens here, what Ari does and she does with him, she must get Felix out—

"—because Minos put me back together. And he's here, he's going to play—"

"You saw Felix? Where is he?"

"In back, by the piano—Wait, who the fuck are you?" finally seeing her, he tries to elbow her aside but "A friend of the family," she says, and grabs that elbow, hooks his ankle, drops him to his knees, calling "Security!" to ID the guards in this tent, flush them out, "security, this person's drunk!" A well-dressed guard, nearly identical to the guests, takes Jason Rice by one arm, a second guard appears—

—but when she turns back to check on Ari, Ari is not where he was, Ari is exiting with the blond doorside greeter, Antwan scampering behind. And the music gets louder, much louder, it echoes in the tent as if echoing from a tomb—

—and Thomas enters from the bunker, gold-seamed tux, black

vest patterned with brocade suns like a fucked-up wizard, a beefy and cartoonishly armed Citadel guard at his side. She angles back, out of his sightline, though Thomas acknowledges no one, greets no one, stares up at the tent's ceiling as if staring at the absent face of God, everyone there might as well be shadows, until "'All observation,'" Thomas says, "'is not just a discovering, but also a bringing forth.' Kierkegaard wrote that. And observation leads to connection. I've put all my resources into this connection . . . Enter into Sunyata."

The Wagner loops, its groaning brass below the guests' excited chatter as they troop after Thomas, but she hangs back, looking between the tent door where Ari has disappeared to the bunker where Felix waits—

—then heads into the cave, its concrete walls smooth and curved like culvert pipes, what was this structure made for, water storage? bombs? And people will pay to hide here, live here? No wonder Thomas chose it for his premiere. She keeps to the crowd's edge until Thomas halts below a slap strip of ceiling spots, pale lights shining on a DJ deck and speakers, a lush incongruous Turkish carpet, an imposing concert grand, *in back, at the piano* but Felix is not here. And as the Wagner dies mid-measure, "Listen to the voice of the divine," Thomas says. "Mr. Felix Perez." Applause begins, she squares up, hands loose—

—but Felix does not appear: the crowd quiets, expectant, then murmuring, questioning, Thomas stares down the tunnel, still no Felix—

—until footsteps, a figure walking out of the emptiness—

—and she knows from the walk that this is Ari: not a swagger, not a march, just a walk, but as confident as that unseen god, he stops on the carpet opposite Thomas and "You wouldn't answer me," Ari says then flashes her a look, brief and very bright, as if something has made him happy, why? "So we came to your party."

And when Thomas starts wiping at his lips, at a widening smile he seems unable to control—it is the single worst expression she has ever seen on Thomas' face—she sights past him, down the tunnel, watching for Felix as "I invited you," Ari says, "to be part of this, I'd still invite you. But you can't own it, even Bergeron knows that. So you can't hear—"

—a sound from the darkness, a machine whine, approaching—and she is running, running into that darkness toward that sound, till yellow safety lights flash on, and she sees it is a maintenance cart with two riders, two men, one in a gold jacket, the other in a pink ballcap. The cart turns abruptly left, down a T-junction, but when she reaches that junction the cart is already gone, past a pair of card-locked double doors—

—and from back up the tunnel she hears a shout, hears the piano's shuddering twang, then an atonal crash, then screams—and she unzips the pocket with the jenny knife and runs back even faster, so fast it feels like being a bullet, so fast that when she hits the Citadel guard head-on she knocks him flat on his back, the guard as he falls sending Thomas sideways into the piano, its polished keyboard smashed, a crack in its smooth wooden side like bone exposed—

—then "Come on—" hustling Ari through the scrum of frightened guests and grim-faced guards and Jason Rice twisting facedown on the carpet, and out to the empty tent and the trike, where "Wait," she says, then throws the trike into reverse, ramming the tent supports so the ferns and flower stands topple and break, the structure itself sags inward, she rams it again and it collapses, blocking the way out—

—and as Ari jumps in, she revs to max speed, racing toward the western treeline, where one of the drone maps revealed a little grassy dip, or gully, behind two tall red pines, not the best or easiest exit, but the closest—

—and suddenly rain, quick drops then a downpour, cold as the wind hits, she hits the retractable roof switch but the roof does not deploy. Rain in her face makes it harder to see, to navigate, the trike slews in the wet grass—but there it is, the pine trees and the gully, deep enough for Ari to crawl and scramble underneath, while she doubles back for Felix—

—but "We're made," Ari says, drenched and hanging on, pointing behind. "They're coming—"

And a human voice this time, "Stop!" from a hood-mounted speaker, two security vehicles gaining on them at a speed this trike can never match, "*Stop!*" so "OK," she says, and drops her grip on the wheel, lets the trike slow and coast to a bumpy halt. "In here they can legally use anything up to deadly force, so don't move. I'll still get us out."

"Don't you move, you're the one they're scared of."

Yet in less than an hour, they sit under foil warming blankets in the site security office, towels draped at their necks, their clips have been returned and "We'll alert you when your transport arrives," says the site security supervisor, a tall woman with a round pink face and a lanyard that reads *Nouvelle Terre Nouvelle Terre.* "Again, our facility apologizes for any misunderstanding."

"My attorney," tapping her clip, "wants to speak to you again."

"Of course. Link it through, please," the supervisor's tone professionally pleasant—

—because everything changed when she did what she had promised herself never to do, told them her name was, is, Basia Grób, and allowed the Grób machinery to activate: the family attorney's calls, the local law enforcement's hands-off stance, the trike arranged to be towed back while a pick-up car has been dispatched, a staffer brought those towels and foil blankets, and bottles of mineral water, and cigarettes for Ari, Marlboro Golds; money is the real law, and in here she has more of it than anyone else.

And when the supervisor leaves, "Look," Ari's nudge, leaning close on the white padded bench, showing her a string of pings—

I said your ass better have an exit strategy, not blow up another party lots of triggers how r u
Social rehab. Jail was better
saving u a smoke

—and "It's Jonas," he says, "Jonas Siegler. I couldn't think of anyone else to call."

"Felix?"

KATHE KOJA

118

"Felix," showing another and still-growing ping string, Unicorn16 with itinerary and ticket confirmation, "Felix should be getting on a plane pretty quick. To New York. You two really need to talk . . . You went in there after him."

"I tried. How did you know?"

"The way you listen to his music. And you put the third seat in the trike."

Looking down at her scar, then into his eyes, later she will ask what happened to get Felix off-site, ruin that piano, cause those screams, but now "It was me," she says. "I gave Antwan Layne your number, I paid for those BIY tickets. Did Felix tell you that? Did Antwan?"

"No. Antwan's not too subtle, but I figured it out myself. Jesus, Ms. Salvay," shaking his head, not angry, "you know you could have just *asked* . . . Was the gallery thing you, too? Meg was upset."

"Only some of it. Mostly it was the Maenads," watching her hand reach for his, take his, their fingers link, and "Ms. Salvay," he says again. "Regina Salve. Basia Gròb."

"Bunny Graves."

"Bunny Gròb."

"Bunny Gròb."

Then a knock, the door opens—"Your transport's here—" the short guard she challenged at the delivery gate, leading them down the white hallway past several other doors—behind one they can hear Jason Rice, shouting, hysterical, "I'm not fucking dangerous, I was having a medical emergency! And being attacked, by you people!"—then opening the last, outer door: as Ari exits, the guard crowds her, to make sure she goes too—

—so she stops, one hand on the jamb, and "Your instincts were good," she says to the guard who leans back in alarm, she lets the foil blanket drop, a crackle of silver at her feet. "But don't feel bad. I always get in."

Then out to the evening's breeze, the rain has passed and the moon is rising, dressed in the last of the clouds, the car is waiting, the gate is open. She says to the gray-suited driver—she told them to send a car with a driver—"Townhouse first, you have that location. Then Indigo Studio," and "Can I smoke in here?" Ari asks, opening the cigarette pack.

And she leans back, into the seat's dark luxury, her luxury now, she feels the water in her boots and the knife in her pocket and the radiating pain in her shoulder from body-checking that Citadel guard, she feels the habit of command like a tool she already knows how to use, to keep safe, to make safe, she feels herself smile: "You can do whatever you want."

"What are you going to do?"

"I'm going to call a board meeting," then to the driver, "Make a stop for coffee on the way."

POLICE REPORT

Case No: 62-89224421

Date: 04/04/2021

Reporting Officer: OFC D.S. Wahner

Incident: Report of aggravated battery, battery, evading arrest

Prepared By: BR/Polizei

Detail of Event:

Ofc responded in Ostern Stn at 2215 4 May 2021 in assist to transit security personnel. Complainant [male cauc 34 yrs] stated that suspect [female cauc 18-20 yrs] reacted negatively to a request to move from a bench. Complainant stated that suspect became aggressive, physically pushed complainant, then struck and kicked complainant several times.

Transit personnel were threatened on approach. When Ofc approached, suspect reacted negatively, then fled. Ofc was unable to secure suspect who remains at large.

Actions Taken:

Complainant statement was taken. Complainant was advised to seek medical aid. Transit personnel were advised to flag suspect within system. Suspect's VI from platform cams and Ofc bodycam has been flagged for further investigation.

TWELVE

Sighting out to the water's foam and swell, Max watches a pirate flotilla chase a dragonboat through a circle of sharks, out where the breakers begin, as a line of players at the water's edge launch their four-masted, spider-rigged lifeboat, one of those groups who band together to finish the game and leave. Beside him, Sergey watches too, until "Anything you want to add," Sergey says, "before we wrap?"

"Did you get everything you needed?"

"I'm good. Last thoughts?"

"Yesterday I saw *Ace or Deuce*."

"You want to talk about *that*? You need to see *Touch the Sky*."

"I just wanted you to know I saw it," and saw there too Sergey's vision, Sergey's eye that looks not through chaos but from deep within it, a bird's eye view in a hurricane: how many people might have filmed that same disastrous opening, but never saw how the spilled cocaine, the director's swinging steel belt buckle, the blue police stickers on the door, made a rebus that told the whole story without saying a single word? "I can see why Ari wanted you to film for him."

"Regon told me once that you always saw what was going to happen before anybody else did."

And he smiles, and shrugs, the praise makes him proud, but melancholy too; he has never heard back from Ari, he finally stopped messaging, the connection they share, had shared, seems over, though he will always be Ari's friend . . . Yet Ari's silence prompted his own last ditch appeal to Mathias, *Ari won't answer, what else can*

I do?—an offer Mathias abruptly accepted, responding not through Clara but directly: Mathias who was, is, the neon octopus in the shallows, always watching with those sharp human eyes, evading the net of corporate identity, and fully fixated on starting over—

Greetings Onionhead! U came back & I will too, not near death NEAR LIFE experience!! Changes everything!!

It can

& u can help me build

Me?

Blocks zeroed out, stamina juiced, now we build, sacrifice good to get best!!!

—and Mathias did have his interblocks removed and usage restored, his life bar fully charges, he can go anywhere now and see anything, interact with any player. When he told Clara, she shook her head in pleased disbelief: *Maybe the HERO fail is a total blessing in disguise. That game just didn't play anyway, I told Matty that to his face.*

What did he say?

He said player fatigue blew it up, he said "Click and Drag killed it twice," whatever that means. And he said he'd help us with CYCLOTRONICA! Simon thinks he's lying but Matty never lies, he never thinks he needs to. Maybe Matty finally found God.

Now from nowhere and everywhere, a sudden voice—"Games are played by entities who need to test a theory, every echo is another door, every door opens and then closes again—" startled to recognize his own voice, detached, almost serene, not at all the way he imagines himself sounding, Sergey pauses the playback audio and "Vondie Berenson really loves your VO," Sergey says. "When she's ready with her cut, she'll ping me, and I'll ping you—Hold up, need to tap in a minute—"

—and while Sergey speaks in that other world, he watches the faraway lifeboat's four masts tilting, wobbling like desperate fingers waving, sinking, the sharks dive then reappear, the water goes calm: those players have left the game, though not the way they intended. Then Sergey says, "Okay, premiere's getting close for *Touch the*

Sky, I'll put you on the list if you want. I really owe you for this, Max, all of this."

He shrugs again, how can Sergey owe him anything? "If you ever come back for a game, let me know."

"And let the goner flies finish me off? It would be cool to shoot those skulls, though, I could spend some serious time here. You interested in that?" and when he nods, "Then let's do it—See you," and Sergey is gone, not flying this time but an instant dissolve, Sergey is no kind of bird anymore, Sergey has left the game too.

Without a reason to stay today, he exits, sitting up straighter at his desk table, feeling the itch of sleeplessness in his eyes, the ache in his shoulders, checking his co-op ride sheet for the day. This week's runs have been a bitch, deliveries are either doubled or scant, sometimes he bikes forty minutes to drop off two boxes of onions and a bag of corn meal, then bikes back to sit waiting out the shift with the other driver; only two of them now, Lincoln was let go, Lincoln yelled about unfair termination but hooked on right away with a Red Dot franchise, the manager said *Red Dot and Lincoln deserve each other.* Today for him looks like another desert day, nothing logged on his sheet—

—but still he feels the need for a ride, so he wheels out, riding to the old Dark Factory street, DREAM HOTEL, and CHEAP BREAKFAST that now is COCKTAILS 24/7, its street-facing windows silvered over, to hide the day from the day drinkers? then passing a Dance Life street demonstration with scarlet sparklers and temple bells, and a sidewalk garden constructed from yellow Sunshine Coffee tins, violet-blue gentians and foamy white phlox, and a mobile Urgent Aid cart that keeps pace with him for a block or two, and Clara's office, though he does not stop there, does not stop anywhere, only rides, feeling the humid afternoon like a ceaseless airborne river, like a constant breath, circular, never-ending—

—and feeling sorry, too, that his time with Sergey is over, it was good to be part of that project, as it was good, much more than good, to be part of Charmi's Yugacycle. But Charmi has not communicated with him, never sent a feather, he never even sees Charmi on the beach, or the paths, anywhere, even with his new parameters, did she block him? He will not check, this silence is her choice, his fault, his loss, he should not have said what he said—though it was true, is still true, *I'm glad you found me,* as happy then as he is now bereft, of Charmi's presence and fervor, of hope to know her better, is all closeness ultimately only loss?

Finally he lets himself slow, stopping for a water refill at a kiosk, he takes out a Good Grape bar—Marfa says *Those bars are basically the peel from the world's driest grape. You should eat more honey*—and sees a new message from Mathias, strange to talk to Mathias as a colleague again, some losses circle back—

Greetings Onionhead, saw your bird friend bounce
You're at Floatsam?
In NYC, greedy insurance fucks, need to fix it. Ever been?
No
Build talk later, find me @ beach

—and he swallows the last of the grape bar with a tepid top-off for his bottle, he had to prime the spigot hard to get the flow: the kiosk pumps are iffy now, some people say the pumps are being made to fail, some people say the city's water system is contaminated, its pipes breached and choked by roots and old backwash. Though Charmi would say *Decay is ultimately generative,* is she finishing her Yugacycle, has she already finished, will he ever see it whole—

—and as if impossibly, miraculously conjured by his longing, a feather appears, curling and uncurling, *ZWIEBEL TALK?* and his heart leaps, then freezes, what should he say to her now? What can he say but YES

MEET AT QUINK?

—the in-game term for the quincunx, where the main paths cross, Mathias calls it the foursquare, again he says YES—then sees where he is, sees the vacant storage building beyond the water kiosk, its walls red with anti-pope and anti-Prophet graffiti, its side lot full of God 4 the People people, one of them is looking his way, then another, the God people are rarely friendly and always unpredictable, so to Charmi *20 RT OK?* because twenty minutes in real time will get him safely back to the dog run park—

20 OK, REALLY GLAD YOU CAN MEET

—and his heart spikes, happy, anxious, he hits the pedals hard to get every bit of his speed, planning nothing to say to her, only to see her, he makes it to the park in fourteen minutes. But his usual bench is full of teenagers pushing and laughing, so he slips under the rusted fence around the old smashball courts, its concrete bisected with determined weeds and puddled brown water—

—to see the quincunx full of golden gingko trees and its paths busy with players—so many, he had no idea how many there really were—crossing, meeting, lingering, green-mouthed explorers and multiarmed builders, skull-climbers, flycatchers, he sees them all but where is she—

—and "Zwiebel," Charmi hopping down from a gingko branch, all her symbols twirling, a little storm of lights. "Zwiebel, hey."

"Charmi," feeling his smile in both worlds, as if his heart is another symbol, flashing and bright. "You're here again."

"I'm always here. I was—collating, it took some time, once I found out about you. And I'm really sorry. And I found Kali, her name's Basia, she owns a drug company."

He has to collate too, instantly bewildered, what to respond to first? "Found out about me?"

"I didn't understand," her frown, not at him, her symbols briefly dim. "I didn't research properly to begin with, so I made assumptions, and I'm sorry. To be blocked like that—"

"Don't be sorry, it's fixed now. I mean don't be sorry anyway, you didn't say anything wrong—"

—as they begin to walk, away from the quink and up one of the paths, not the shining one to the skulls but a winding and mainly secluded track through insistent serpent bushes, then a quiet flowering rest-meadow, then up again, to a quartz pink promontory jutting out over a narrow valley, where below sits a small circular structure, also pink, with what could be arms, is it a statue? a playscape, a dwelling? has it always been there? And he sees the breezy ruffle of her pelt, her rangy grace against the rocks, like thought arrayed against time, her blue, blue eyes—

"—when I *did* research, I got to Mathias Bergeron. That led to Dark Factory, then Kuntsfarm, 'Buttercup'—"

"'Buttercup,' how did you find out about—"

"—and Marla, wait, Marfa Carpenter. She has a very extensive archive, really detailed, it's called 'Making It Real.' But she wouldn't give me access, or meet with me here—"

Charmi and Marfa, when worlds collide. "She doesn't like it in here."

"—and when she did agree to an Aura meet, she was really rude."

"But why did you want to learn all that?"

"Because I—I wanted to know what happened, how it happened. To you, Zwiebel," her gaze to his, and he sees that she was not offended, she did not leave, she wanted, she wants—"But when I was collating, I saw that I have it all basically backward. The stories about the gods are stories about the avatars, the people who turn the wheel, so I need to reframe the whole Yugacycle through the avatars. Rework it all," her scholar's mind unafraid to start again, sacrifice good to get best, yes, and "If I can help," he says, "with the Yugacycle, or anything—Anything you do, Charmi—"

"I'd be glad. Really glad—Down there," pointing to the pink glow far below, "the stupa, it's where I work. Want to see?"

And the evening's cloudy sunset is that same quartz pink, the greenish streetlights like strung stars, as he takes the day's last ride, all the way uptown, to the farthest end of the park, where the farmers' market stands used to be, and the building where Ari had once been an emperor, the Holy Roman Empire, its lease sign unreadably old, its metal doors rusted shut, one looks broken open. A cargo van is parked just past that building, HIVE MIND stenciled in yellow on one side, and Marfa sits in its passenger seat, frowning through an Aura. And he smiles, remembering the first time he saw her, her brash vitality, the chopped swing of her chestnut hair, KACTUS KWEEN hoodie and her small warm hand, *We definitely need to talk more—*

—as she powers down the van window and "Haven't seen you in a minute," she says, as he dismounts. "Following up on your girlfriend? The blonde?"

Girlfriend—Charmi is blonde? "You mean Charmi?"

"Right, Charmian, the ghost from your game. She hit me up about you, but myths, gods, that's not my business," Marfa clearly, deeply annoyed, why? "I did tell her you were never the same after Dark Factory . . . Anyway," a brisk dismissive shrug, "I just found out that the city's going to tear down that building there. So the hives are going to have to move."

"Move where?"

"Don't know. Our fundraising failed on launch."

"Where's Pavel?"

She points to a scrub patch just beyond that building, a fence of warped pallets lashed neatly together, a lunar-suited figure moving between square white wooden boxes—"He's treating for mites—" and as he approaches, Pavel turns, tugging off the medieval cloaking headgear, Pavel looks surprised but makes a smile.

"Hello, Max. Marfa is in the van."

"I know. I came to talk to you," but finds it hard to start, they stand in awkward silence as tiny, busy bodies float around them, homing back to the hives, until "I had a place, once," he says, "for a show. Then the woman who owned the property sold it to a corporation."

"That's quite sad. The land, you know, it's so difficult to get."

"I actually wanted to have bees in that show, but Teresa—Anyway," why not just say what he came here to say? that selling his B of P shares brought money he does not need, will never need, so what better use than—"I just bought the property back," the trees and little stream still surprisingly unruined, or maybe ruin was always its meaning, its brown beauty and windblown trash, its emptiness untouched by any loss. "And I want to give it to you. For the hives. Marfa's been there, she can tell you what it's like."

"You—" Pavel's face turns red, redder, is Pavel upset? "Marfa asked you for this?"

"No."

"She knows about it?"

"No. But Marfa's been a good friend to me, so this property would be like a thank you to her, if you accept it. Just let me know what you want to do."

Climbing back on his bike, he sees Pavel hurrying to the van, leaning into the window as Marfa leans out, he waves to both but neither see him—

—and he rolls off into this new night like the twilight of the gods, change and ruin are already fully in process, but if shared loss is more painful than bearing it alone, could it also be more conducive to growth? or even a joined part of that process, like the ring around his finger, ouroboros—

—and the feather floating into his view, *ZWIEBEL SEND PAGES*, the pages he once thought he was writing for Ari, the pages that Charmi now will read, and use, they will use all of it together: canon, lore, apocrypha, death, love, time, *dum vivimus vivamus, the gods have to live somewhere,* all one story because every god has one, every world is one, telling itself to itself through every playable day.

TUTTO BENE, IT'S ALL JUST A WALK IN THE PARK:

ARTS ENTREPRENEUR MEGHAN SORIN AND DIRECTOR SERGEY KENDRICKS FIND THEMSELVES IN CHAOS

SIMON CHERRY

Q: Sergey Kendricks, you've exploded onto the film scene with your wild documentary *Touch the Sky*, it's being shown at all the fests, it's winning all the awards, Grete Folsker at *Neue Kino* calls you a "visionary." And Meghan Sorin, you're a respected veteran of the entertainment world. So how did you two meet?

SK: Have to credit that one to [producer Ari] Regon.

MS: We officially met through the Dark Park performance. Ari was a very early admirer of Sergey's work.

Q: *Touch the Sky* throws its viewers into a maelstrom of fans chasing, crying, and ultimately rioting over a performer. Your new project, *Artemis*, explores a volatile, sometimes violent, arts group, or gang, called the Bridesmaids. Is it fair to classify you both as crisis connoisseurs?

MS: That would be a bit reductionist.

SK: Well a crisis is full of energy, a crisis is a turning point. And people's lives definitely changed during *Touch the Sky*—we've been hearing stories from all type of people, powerful stories. We hope for the same energy with *Artemis*.

Q: Will the sculptor Suze Duplantier be involved in that film?

SK: We reached out to her, but—

MS: At this stage it's premature to discuss anyone's involvement.

Q: Do you think chaos, or danger, is necessary to make interesting art?

SK: Vision is what's necessary. But we know situations can become, call it volatile. So we prepare for that.

Q: Your own lives have changed because of these projects. Your production companies have merged, you share offices in the old Vitrina complex, you appear together on industry panels and at social events. So have your personal lives merged too?

SK: Work is how we live. And working with Meghan is the honor of my life.

MS: Sergey can always make a space for us to breathe, wherever we are.

Q: What would you say to viewers who are just being introduced to your collaboration?

SK: Keep your eyes open.

MS: Remember to breathe.

goodbye doubts goodbye hubris goodbye heroes

say goodbye to it all at the

GOODBYE WORLD BALL

Music by FREGON
wsg Fuxury –
Code Riddle –
Escalanta – NYC NIA

Streaming live from
Alphabet City NYC

Come & celebrate the
new Dandelion Field in
Birds of Paradise

THIRTEEN

Coming 2 premiere?

try 2 4 sure

Save you a seat, smoking bar

And Ari smiles to Meghan through his Aura: "Thought Sergey said he quit smoking?"

"He did," her shrug, Meg in a draping bark-brown hoodie, a long room with long windows, workstations and a spiky green line of ferns, AWIP has a new office, AWIP is partnered with Tutto Bene now. "But between *Touch the Sky* and starting up *Artemis,* he's a bit pressured."

"How about you?"

"I haven't started smoking, no," with the smile he remembers, the amusement and calm: Meg is past the sad stress of Suze, and the distrust of Insomnious—though she refuses to warm up to Bunny; Uni will not either—and the Maenads' stalking craziness has now turned, through Sergey's focus, to a fearsome energy, impossible not to want to watch. He has seen a few clips from that gallery footage, Meg sent them, *I never wanted to look at any of this again, but Sergey asked me over and over, he said you can't let it all end here.* "Ness will choose the Maids—you remember Ness, from the café? Ness believes what happened at the gallery is not what the Maids are about, we've had some very long talks. Now I'm trying to confirm the location shoot dates. Ilias is quite scattered—"

"Illy is spaced. He prays a lot."

"—but Gus Burns is responsive, so we should be out there soon."

"The woods are the same, only muddier," those woods where Meg danced, and the little lake beyond, where Felix swam . . . No one asks him about Felix, why Felix is staying in New York and he is here, though he knows they all wonder. "When you firm it up, let me know."

"I will. Oh, and Antwan Layne contacted AWIP again, using your name—he's persistent. And unbearable."

"He is," and even worse than before because Antwan is over asking questions, is only demand, open hands grabbing at vacuum, at a throwaway "interview" in Zipper, at whatever he thinks will make him whatever he thinks Felix is. Yet Antwan was unexpectedly useful at Tom Hae's doomsday show, Antwan was the three-minute distraction the doorway greeter needed, hot blond Denis who found then scrambled into a maintenance cart, to ferry Felix out of that bunker, out to the compound's main entrance—he had Uni park a backup driver there, to get Felix to the airport, whatever Tom Hae had planned was nothing he wanted Felix to be part of: cold piano, cold tunnel, cold as a grave . . . Antwan thought he was helping to send Felix away for good, Antwan was gleeful, *Don't chase a dude, replace a dude!* Antwan just as ready to ditch his evening's date, Jase the event company barback—Jason Rice who took all the blame for his own veto of MinosLAB, because Tom Hae wanted someone to punish, so Jase needed someone to hate—Antwan said *I know he doesn't vibe with you, and everybody on Dive says he's always junked on sizzy, but for real Jase knows a ton of industry players.*

And you know Bunny. How did that happen?

And the look on Antwan's face was all the confirmation he needed—though really he needed none, it made sense no other way, Antwan having his number, Antwan's expensive BIY invitation, Antwan's slip at Meg's party—but *She said to keep my mouth shut,* Antwan in a kind of panic, *don't let her beat me up!*

No one tells her what to do. But she won't do it today. Just tell me how—

—because the why of it she had already told him herself, *I want to make things happen with you, everything, volume, volume,* the smoke and her smile and her blood, she risked herself to save him, she meant every word—though she never meant or tried or wanted to take Felix's place, she knows Felix is part of him, knows it better than Felix does—

—and she knew how to get him away from Tom Hae's smile, there in that tunnel, when he told Tom Hae *You can't hear what Felix is playing, you can't hear Felix at all*—said not to be cruel but to be clear, very clear, about the terms of meeting Tom Hae's triggered need, what would have happened then if Tom Hae knew Felix was already gone?

But instead Jase happened, Jase bursting in like an anime Quirk ad, waving some rod or bat or maybe something snatched from behind the bar, Jase swung it, at him? at Tom Hae? but hit the piano instead, an odd and terrible sound, as if something alive had been beaten, Jase screamed *You prick!* and hit the piano again. The Citadel goon aimed a sloppy bar brawl punch that completely missed as the site guards arrived with shocksticks, when Jase hit the carpet the Citadel goon kicked him in the neck and Jase started spasming, convulsing, the guests really started screaming then. And then Bunny was back and they were gone, the trike and the rain and the Gród Chemie EUV, Bunny is at her board meeting right now—

—and "Don't hire Antwan," he says to Meg, "for anything. But I sent you a linki for Denis."

"The event greeter, yes, he's gorgeous, we can put him on the door at the premiere. Try to come, Ari. It would mean the world to Sergey."

He smiles and kisses two fingers to her—"Try my best, for you—" then ends the call, and calls out to Gus who is crossing from the main room into the studio, cords looped in one hand, bent blunt in the other, "Hey, you think Addam can give me a ride over to the townhouse?"

"Sure. They're out back, I think—"

—and at that back door, he pauses to stroke Andromeda who

pauses for him, rubs her sleek small head against his knuckles, then slips into the studio and "She sits and waits," Gus says, "for him, she misses him. We all do."

Outside, he sees Addam out by the ancient truck chassis, rusted down to its armature now, like a beast gone finally to bones: he takes his time walking over, through the green and seeding weeds, down a path made by years of people heading to the woods, or to the lake, he takes out a cigar but does not light it, pauses beneath the crabapple trees to pick one of the small hard apples, shaped almost like a heart, he cups it in his palm. Something, more apples rotting? some other death? lies soft and too sweet by his feet, in the grass, and the wind moves through that grass like the sound of a hushing crowd, just after the lights go down . . . Two days ago Jonas called him, Jonas with a buzz cut that looks strange but not bad, Jonas asked *You still in Asscrack Europa? Not too many clubs out there.*

It's really pretty out here. And I don't need a club.

You're a maker. You need to get busy.

I am busy. But sometimes you need to unmake, first—

Right, you're a philosopher now?

"As big as it gets," you said that, remember? That's how big this is, it's so big it doesn't need anything but itself.

*Yeah, you're a philosopher. Or it's the blunts—*And when he laughed, a real laugh, Jonas smiled, a serious smile and *Your fucking brain, Ari, I told you that a long time ago.*

Legal issues keep Jonas tethered in place, so when Bergeron's staffer sent another guest list ping, he pinged back **Just Ms. Grób & Ava Perez**, his guests for Bergeron's GOODBYE WORLD BALL, the official announcement party for a new sub-game inside *Birds of Paradise*, where Felix's music will play nonstop; Bergeron says Felix offered to play the party too, is that why the party is in New York? Clara Dix is involved, with Aaron and Na Ja, and Insomnious gifted him Geraldine and her team with a temporary waiver, because Insomnious had a trickier ask for him, Uni sent it on—

Offer is C-suite, title TBD but "creative leadership"
upgrade 2 Hae 2.0? pass
Salary is your call
pass
Good call imo

And *They're just glad I tanked the platform before they bled out,* he told Bunny, shaking his head; while she travels she calls him every few days, she calls it her off-site security check. *But an offer like this means Hae's permanently AWOL, he'd never work with me again. Wonder where he is.*

At the Last Supper? Bergeron out-crazied him on that one. And Insomnious is on my list, I'll tell you more when I get back.

How's your trip going?

Very productive. Tomorrow I'm going to deal with my fucking grandmother.

Now he is close enough on the path to hear Addam, Addam kneeling, tapping that bare chassis, with what? a little hammer, a piano tuning hammer, here, then there, when they spot him watching they pause and "The tones you can get with this," Addam says, "the resonance, it's amazing. Felix showed me how."

On the drive to the townhouse Addam does not speak, and neither does he, only watches the world go by—slowly, everybody's driving seems slow after Bunny's—and listens to Addam's mix, pounding then snaking then rising, rolling from Upsetta to Ded Mann to Model 500, then to Felix, then "That mask," he says to Addam, as they pull in past the fence yard, busy as ever, crime does pay. "The Minos mask. You want it?"

"What?"

"It's up in the guest room, by the bed," next to his own old ancient black hoodie, both sent on by Max; only Max would send it, only Max would remember to send the hoodie too. "If you want it, it's yours."

"That's—That's fucking *iconic*," with happy awe. "Thank you, tell Felix thank you! Tell him I'll keep it safe."

Inside the townhouse is very quiet, it smells like coffee and faint smoke and even fainter cherry hair pomade. When Bunny left on her warrior's campaign, she left her own space military-neat; his, his and Felix's, is a mess, ashtray and scattered cups, kicked-off boots and plum silk robe, unused hand weights and rumpled bedsheets that should be changed, but they smell like Felix, Felix's faded Indigo t-shirt lies on their bed, it smells like Felix too, he sleeps in that shirt every night . . . *This is our home. Or do you miss New York?* He misses Felix.

Up on the roof to smoke, he feels the sun's reach through the thin clouds, like a blessing almost arrived, and thinks of the caged-in mezzanine at Peitsche, *Estoy vivo bebé,* those two sleepless days like a year's worth, a lifetime's worth of concept and production, culmination: at Peitsche he saw the triggers so naked in display, saw the humble, stumbling, awful human needs so clearly that it changed the anger and pain of Felix's distrust, alchemized it to a clarity, a pure surety, he knew what to do then, about everything—

—about the bunker show too, he never saw Felix there, or pinged beforehand to explain, he gave Denis a kiss on the cheek and said *Give him that, and tell him Ari says You need to go right now.* And that night, later, very late, Felix finally pinged him, no words, not even music, only ten sweet seconds of his face, his gaze all yearning, but resolute, about to enter the New York airport's rush.

And even later, almost morning when he lay down, he slept and he dreamed, the same dream of the empty hallway, and miles of scrawled white walls, and the man he chases laughing as he laughs back, call and response—until finally he stood looking out a window so dark he could see nothing at all, the absolute darkness of ruin and what comes after, then heard that laugh again, from right behind him—and turning, he saw himself, not like a mirror but like an answer, wild hair and wide smile, *model's smile,* and he woke, and rubbed his face, and laughed again.

Now he looks down at the trees and the courtyard and the gravel road that leads to the whole world, decentralized, eternal, already in process, like dandelions shivering with seeds: all of it his platform, not made with power or force, not a nameless space constructed from specs and money—though the work of constructing it was very real, its makers too, and they will have more work to do—but instead from that rusted chassis and waving weeds, and the roses and bottles on the Factory floor, the fucking at Silver Landings and the fighting at Quest Fest, the silent church in Barcelona and the dancefloor masses and the Beat Shack graduation, the hunger at Peitsche and the ask from Insomnious, all of that is his to work with, make with, what else did Jonas say? *You get them to do whatever you want,* and what he wants is to keep it all spinning, eternally moving, all it needed was a breath of air to start.

And in the game that is not named *HERO,* that add-on to Paradise, Bergeron will stream the music and the students will learn the music and Felix will play the music, and his gift, his breath will keep working for Felix, always, together or apart. Because there is one lesson left to learn, his own fear of loss long dissolved, but Felix still needs to find a way to trust; till then he will wait.

After this night's work—nothing to turn blue over, as Uni always says, a half-dozen meetings on Argot, a Belgian festival team wanting him to consult on their UX, and the most promising, and interesting, a new social platform called Tussle, an irresistible two-line ask, *If Ari Regon was starting out right now, he'd be on Tussle. Will you meet?*—he pays one of the young fence yard guys for a ride to the Outpost: soccer jersey and two gold rings, one says DA, one says FUCK, and "You getting that breakfast slice, huh?" the fence guy says, jerking the truck to a stop before the curry and pizza shop, the clinic and pharm are just opening their doors. "Hey—That Miss Boots, where's she at?"

"She'll be back. Thanks," then into the clinic, to the clean and narrow tattoo booth where the lanky angel wing artist who inked his stars is long gone, but a burly man with a biker Virgin Mary on one arm greets him, seats him, and "You're Bruni," nodding to the man. "Everybody says you do amazing scar work."

"Out here I do a lot. Clinic's got the serum treatment too."

"I don't want to hide it," pulling off his shirt, "I want something added—" *SEE AGAIN THE STARS*, Bunny told him that quote, she said it in Italian, *E quindi uscimmo a riveder le stelle, Then we came forth, to see again the stars,* and "If you don't want it covered," Bruni's big gloved exploratory hands very gentle on his skin, "we for sure can make it part of the art."

Afterward, as he sits outside the Outpost bar, a takeout Red Rose whiskey in hand to take the edge off the needling, tingling pain, there is a ping: Felix, shirtless in the old dim New York apartment, with a rosy, fresh tattoo, black letters above the dandelions on his chest, at his heart, *JE T'AIME BÉBÉ*. And seeing it, he blinks, the tears sudden and warm, he pings back **show u mine**

—and back at the townhouse again, he does, tugging off the derm wrapping, angling his clip, no answer at first from Felix but he is patient, the bedroom quiet around him, their bedroom, their house, their home—

—then the long and passionate string, Felix's relief, and grief, what Felix feared, always feared, and always needed, **You did everything 4 me, everything, but I wanted u 2 need me, same way I need u**

want u more than anything

king always a king, they all want u!! but ur not "mine" music's not "mine" beats not "mine" Mrs G used 2 say it's a gift from God & we don't choose

♥♥♥

I told my mom & she said Oh u messed WAY up & need 2 say sorry, I'm sorry baby never ever again

♥♥♥ ♥♥♥

Made a song 4 you, vintage remix, my mom & dad used 2 dance 2 it, they were in love 4ever

like us

my baby

my star

—with a line of kisses, kisses sent back that he feels in his body, Felix's body bare in that room, the hunger of separation almost as steep as the joy—

KATHE KOJA

140

—and the next ping is from Bergeron's onsite lieutenant, confirming arrival, and the ping after that is Uni, and after that no ping but wheels on the gravel and feet on the stairs, boots, quick and "Knock knock," from Bunny at the door, Bunny in her mycelium vest, silver Dargon shades on a long silver chain, a tiny new silver nose ring: she looks stunning, like a brand-new weapon, she is smiling her wide red smile and "Air trike's ready," she says. "Time to go to the ball."

WAKE UP THE WILLING GODS —THE RIG VEDA

FOURTEEN

There are certain corporate perks she has forgotten existed, and instant mobility is near the top of that list: vehicles of any kind are always ready to take her wherever she wants to go—like this plane, where Ari sips white wine and chats with the flirtatious cabin attendant, now the cabin attendant is showing Ari his forearm tattoo, a boring sunflower—and the quiet, impregnable EUV that took her to the victorious board meeting, and the smaller, even quieter sedan that followed the winding road up to the private aerie that is Blue Mountains, the care facility, though no one at Blue Mountains calls it that, they call it "the residence."

Agni is in residence there, Agni propped on a private terrace, blue sky, white birds, green fir trees, it reminded her of Thomas' fake castle backgrounds, but all of it is real, and beyond expensive, just like Agni's sickness. She did not bother to learn the full nature of that sickness or its many failed treatments, only enough to know that it was escalating, painful, and fatal; she spoke as briefly as possible to Agni's nursing care manager, she knew that manager found her crisp and uncaring, the manager was right. But the manager could not have known that her heart was beating the way it used to beat before a match, fast, ready for violence, needing the violence—

—and *I just spoke to your nurse,* she said, advancing onto that terrace like taking enemy territory, she looked first at the lovely view then down at Agni: not smaller but shrunken in the wheelchair, caved in by the pain, a chic pixie cut and yellow silk robe, oxygen cannula and papaya juice in a glass on the glass table beside her; ZZ's hospital room was nowhere near as nice, or clean, or deserved.

He's concerned you're on the verge of opiate toxicity, and all those benzos don't help. Too bad Grób Chemie can't come up with something better.

Basia, and Agni stared at her, the same stare, no change there. *Did you come to watch me suffer?*

No, to show you something, turning her clip to display the drone footage of the Arles apartment's demolition, white marble chunks and fresh brown dirt, the shine of broken glass, she clicked through to the legal *permis de démolir* and *The planning authority was fairly cheap to persuade. I gave the go myself on the wrecking ball.*

You evil, spiteful—

I did it for Mama, and for ZZ, but she would not speak ZZ's name in that place. *Want to watch it again?*

That apartment belonged to the family, and Agni raised her hand, shaking with anger's palsy: her sapphire ring was gone, the one that used to leave a mark. *I did everything I could to rid the family of you—*

I was the one who stole your Vuitton board, those lessons useful in more than one way, back checkers first, always clear from the rear, never double too early, never play for more than you're willing to lose: she has never, ever played to lose. *And I'm the family now, I'll be restructuring the company,* taking from it everything she needs for everything she plans to do—full support for whatever Ari does next, and next, and next, and a DJ school if Felix wants that, and legal aid to help people pinned the way ZZ was pinned, and then Insomnious, she knows enough from Thomas to know Insomnious can be useful—while she hurls a permanent spanner into the global pharma works, she has some very busy years ahead. *The board agrees we need a younger hand on the wheel.*

If I live until the end of this year—Your cousin Bettina is a Grób—

You won't live two more months. And Bettina's only seventeen. I just took her boot shopping.

I suppose you think you've won. I suppose you'll scatter my ashes in your wasteland, to spite me—

*Someone else will deal with that—*as she leaned in like the hand of God, the smell of spilled papaya juice, of Agni's sour wetness, Agni's rotten old soul and *You tried to make me hate life,* she said, *but I'm happy now. I fucking know I won.*

At the balcony's periphery stood several flower arrangements, tasteful white asters and trailing vines, all sent from business entities, no human heart involved. She snapped one aster stem and sent it sailing over the railing, in lieu of throwing Agni herself, then thanked the care manager and climbed back into the quiet sedan.

And before she left the Gròb Chemie headquarters and its overnight executive suite—a soothing view of city lights and the lines of the treeless mountains, a tea bar and cold plunge and sauna, another handy perk—she heard from Thomas, a nighttime call, voice only: *Bunny?*

Thomas. I didn't think we'd talk again.

Are you with Ari Regon, now?

Right now I'm alone.

He's a dreadful person, Bunny. But so are you, Thomas' voice clear yet very far away, not unhinged but adrift, somewhere where no one else was; as bad as he looked at that bunker event, his voice was even worse, like that inner void, squirming and hissing. *All people are. Small and dreadful, and filled with the devil's petty wisdom—Except for Mr. Perez. He would have brought the voice, I'm certain of that, I had everything in place. But to be accused of simony! Of trying to buy God—*

I know what simony is. Where are you, Thomas?

"It is said that the world is empty, the world is empty, lord." Connection is the only real currency—

—then a sound, not loud, a little crack, a thump, *Thomas?* but he did not answer, she waited, finally the call timed out. In a day or two the News Immediate cycle briefly featured *Insomnious Group executive found dead,* the spin was assault, a home invasion, authorities were reviewing the Citadel security footage; Insomnious must have been relieved, suicide means no termination payout for Thomas' estate. And Thomas finally got what he wanted.

Now they are descending through cloudless skies, the flight attendant gathering their glasses, "Hope you have a wonderful visit to New York, Mr. Regon," then quick through the customs concierge, the first person she sees is Bergeron's driver, black yoga pants and a t-shirt with an old-school spinning Y globe, the driver beckoning, "This way, please—" And then a pink ballcap and blush roses, Felix waiting, Felix looks more beautiful than she has ever seen him, Felix is aglow and "Baby," Felix says, seeing only Ari. "My baby—"

—so she swings her travel bag onto her shoulder, and heads into the city alone.

And nothing has changed, everything has changed, she has changed: the smoke shops and cafés and gated restaurants are still there, if less crowded and more makeshift, and the sun seems hotter, she must be used to the townhouse rain. But the pedestrians still part for her, the security guards still watch her pass, and she still goes fastest on foot—first to check out the site for the Goodbye World party, a literal old ballroom slated to be razed, but saved by Bergeron's last-minute interest, the streets around it are less than ideal but they will be safe enough, and inside it looks like a half-trashed clubhouse, an eccentric's collection of disco balls and an extremely high-end sound system. Next she heads to the gallery where the Bridesmaids once brought havoc, to offer her patronage, and ease any qualms over Meghan Sorin's upcoming film—that will please Ari—then stops to buy more lipstick, Carna Purest Red, before taking her gown to the couture bridal cleaners who promise to have it "Rush-ready by this evening, certainly. Where shall we have it sent?" so she gives them the address of the Insomnious satellite office, she still has the codes for that, she gave that address to the tailor too.

And as the sun begins its fall, orange heat to blue-gray twilight, the streets still radiating warmth, Ari pings *drinks 1st?* so she pings back *my treat* then crosses the bridge to meet them at a dark-walled dive called Albert's Hole, pausing a moment in the doorway, how will Felix react to her—

—but already Ari is waving, making space at a dim corner two-top, its lacquer scratched with a palimpsest bible of love, hate, fucking, and random numbers, and "Champagne here, thanks," Ari says to the server, a twig of a boy with butterscotch curls, then to Felix and to her, "Play nice."

That makes Felix smile, she smiles too and "He told me," Felix says, "about that kebab shop, how you kept him safe. That job's never done, trust me."

"The shop owner said they ID'd us," from the discarded Pflaume Thé bottle, DNA ID, she is in multiple databases for multiple reasons, and Ari's apparently came from some kid misdemeanor, trespassing in a club. "He said he was going to press robbery charges—"

"Robbery? Listen, she literally threw cash at the fucking guy—"

"—so I told him if he did, I'd come back and make him eat that bottle."

Felix gives her a look, the way he used to look at her over the backgammon board. "You catch more flies with honey than with broken glass."

"Well, how many flies do we need?"

"Once a guy pointed a gun at Felix during one of his sets, at a dive just like this one—"

"Way worse than this one," Felix says, then to her, only to her, "What we were playing, was that the money game?"

"No," watching his gaze, no anger there, only the wariness that comes after attack. "No, it wasn't. And it wasn't fair, you didn't know what game we were really playing."

"It was your game. But I made it way easy for you—"

"You folks here are the champagne?" the server approaching with a festive cheap prosecco, Ari takes the bottle and makes the toast—"To my two favorite people in the world—" and she touches her glass first to Felix's, Felix touches his glass to hers, they all drink. Then "He used to call you my girlfriend," Felix says. "So okay. A big sister, I can deal with that."

As they finish the bottle, the cleaners ping the delivery on her ballgown, and she shows it to them, strapless parachute silk and blue as midnight, and "That's spectacular," Ari says. "Creative black tie! I should have got a suit from Bodley Pearce."

Felix makes a face at the name, and she laughs—"I had your sizes, still, from Peitsche, I got you a suit. A sea wool tux, from Zhang Hopper—" and that name makes Felix whistle: "You got him a real Zhang Hopper?" then to Ari, "There's a mile-long waiting list for a suit like that."

"Not for her," Ari says.

As Felix leaves for soundcheck, with a kiss for Ari, and a nod for her—"I'll play you two a walk-on song—" she and Ari take a company car, her car, to the Insomnious building—

—where the security guard does not ask her to thumbsign for the deliveries, the lobby trash can is visibly grubby and full, and the ninth floor is emptier, fewer door plaques, no more rubber plant, all the hallway lights are random, mostly staying dark. The office door has no new signage, the mountain graphic is gone, and Ari says "Talk about goodbye world."

She is pleased to see the tux fits him just as it should, of course it is a Zhang Hopper, and the Cobblers' Row tailor is impeccable even without a dedicated fitting. And Ari is impressed by the cufflinks she offers, pigeon's blood rubies, antique and perfect—salvaged from the Arles apartment, let something good come out of that ruin—Ari admires their gleam, tweaks his cuffs, smooths back his hair, then "I better glam up," he says, and sits at the receptionist's station with a tiny bottle of polish, moss green glitter Glam Bam polish, and carefully paints his nails; ZZ used to wear that brand too.

In the lav she applies fresh lipstick, and adjusts the gown's décolleté, she knows she looks spectacular—then feels a flaring impulse, mysterious, playful, and digs around in the travel bag to find and free the Maenad crown—why is it here, and not at the townhouse? She does not remember packing it, was it in the bag all this time? but in that cold and lunar bathroom light she settles it on her head, tilts it, it fits, it belongs to her.

When she steps back into the office, boots clicking, silk rustling, Ari whistles—"Well hello, goddess—" and together they process down the empty hallway, waiting for the balky elevator, waiting, and "Here," she says, and dabs a pinky's worth of lipstick on the curve of his smile; she smiles too; the elevator doors open.

Now the lobby is empty, no guard, maybe the man there before was not a guard at all. Outside the car waits, its lights dimmed in the dark, its passenger door swinging wide on the glowing blue-lit interior as they exit the building: and Ari pauses, to let her manage her skirts, and enter first—

—but a sudden body, colliding, wrenching at them—"Hey!"—a white man in a red windbreaker, snatch and grab, grabbing for what? Ari's clip? her crown? so she grabs that man, fast and brutal, flips and trips him to the sidewalk, lifts her boot then "Siktir git!" she snaps, and lets him scramble up and away—

—and to Ari "All right?" as he lets out a breath, takes a breath, nods: "With you? Always."

Then into the car and "Drive," she says: down the street, to the corner, the avenue, the bridge, the venue, the ball that says goodbye to one world to start another rolling, just like death, just like myth, just like love. And "'Love in action,'" she says, watching the streets pass, some with traffic, some with people, some with nothing at all, "'is a harsh and dreadful thing, compared to love in dreams.'"

"Who said that?"

"I don't remember."

He lights a cigar, one of the last of the ones she sent him, and they share it, they exit the car bathed in its smoke, to climb the cracking concrete steps arm in arm, her silk and his rubies, his smile and her crown, under the shiny pink and teal GOODBYE banners, passing through the other partygoers in couture leather and pink puffy skirts and white and silver Bridesmaids outfits and t-shirts from games she has never seen or heard of, wearing Auras and Quirks, carrying flowers, turning clips on them, following them, what is the quote about calling to the celebration everyone from the streets and the city? as many here already as this building will hold—

—and "Listen," she says, because Felix is already playing, she knows his music, would know it anywhere—*they never wanted me to stop, I couldn't handle it then* but now he can, now Felix has what he needs—and this music is made for them, for her, a walk-on song, a woman's commanding voice and a beat that drives the stars, *Stars when you shine, freedom is mine, I know how I feel—*

My great and continuing gratitude to

Christopher Schelling, always
Carter Scholz
Charlie Athanas
Aaron Mustamaa
Rick Lieder
and to Tricia Reeks especially

—Kathe Koja

KATHE KOJA writes immersive fiction and creates and produces live and virtual experiences. Reach her at kathe@darkfactory.club

ARI REGON is a producer who loves to dance.

MAX CASPAR is a reality artist, game theorist and developer, and full-time cyclist.

FELIX PEREZ is a musician.

SERGEY KENDRICKS is a documentary filmmaker and founder of Tutto Bene Productions. His films include *Touch the Sky*, *Ace or Deuce*, and the upcoming *Artemis*. His work has won the Creative Imaging Award, the Iris Foundation's Outstanding Documentary Award, and the New Vision Fellowship.

BUNNY GRAVES is a freelance relationship auditor.

CHARMIAN DUGLASS/CHARMSKOOL is a classicist and chaos scholar, with a focus on gaming and systems collapse.